THE DUELING MACHINE

THE DUELING MACHINE

BENJAMIN WILLIAM BOVA,
MYRON R. LEWIS

ISBN: 978-93-5342-810-5

First Published: -

LECTOR HOUSE LLP
E-MAIL: lectorpublishing@gmail.com

THE DUELING MACHINE

BY

BEN BOVA
AND
MYRON R. LEWIS

The trouble with great ideas is that someone is sure to expend enormous effort and ingenuity figuring out how to louse them up.

ILLUSTRATED BY
JOHN SCHOENHERR

CONTENTS

THE DUELING MACHINE

CHAPTER I

Dulaq rode the slide to the upper pedestrian level, stepped off and walked over to the railing. The city stretched out all around him—broad avenues thronged with busy people, pedestrian walks, vehicle thoroughfares, aircars gliding between the gleaming, towering buildings.

And somewhere in this vast city was the man he must kill. The man who would kill him, perhaps.

It all seemed so real! The noise of the streets, the odors of the perfumed trees lining the walks, even the warmth of the reddish sun on his back as he scanned the scene before him.

It is an illusion, Dulaq reminded himself, *a clever man-made hallucination. A figment of my own imagination amplified by a machine.*

But it seemed so very real.

Real or not, he had to find Odal before the sun set. Find him and kill him. Those were the terms of the duel. He fingered the stubby cylinderical stat-wind in his tunic pocket. That was the weapon he had chosen, his weapon, his own invention. And this was the environment he had picked: his city, busy, noisy, crowded, the metropolis Dulaq had known and loved since childhood.

Dulaq turned and glanced at the sun. It was halfway down toward the horizon, he judged. He had about three hours to find Odal. When he did—kill or be killed.

Of course no one is actually hurt. That is the beauty of the machine. It allows one to settle a score, to work out aggressive feelings, without either mental or physical harm.

Dulaq shrugged. He was a roundish figure, moon-faced, slightly stooped shoulders. He had work to do. Unpleasant work for a civilized man, but the future of the Acquataine Cluster and the entire alliance of neighboring star systems could well depend on the outcome of this electronically synthesized dream.

He turned and walked down the elevated avenue, marveling at the sharp sensation of hardness that met each footstep on the paving. Children dashed by and rushed up to a toyshop window. Men of commerce strode along purposefully, but without missing a chance to eye the girls sauntering by.

I must have a marvelous imagination, Dulaq thought smiling to himself.

Then he thought of Odal, the blond, icy professional he was pitted against. Odal was an expert at all the weapons, a man of strength and cool precision, an emotionless tool in the hands of a ruthless politician. But how expert could he be with a stat-wand, when the first time he saw one was the moment before the duel began? And how well acquainted could he be with the metropolis, when he had spent most of his life in the military camps on the dreary planets of Kerak, sixty light-years from Acquatainia?

No, Odal would be lost and helpless in this situation. He would attempt to hide among the throngs of people. All Dulaq had to do was to find him.

The terms of the duel restricted both men to the pedestrian walks of the commercial quarter of the city. Dulaq knew the area intimately, and he began a methodical hunt through the crowds for the tall, fair-haired, blue-eyed Odal.

And he saw him! After only a few minutes of walking down the major thoroughfare, he spotted his opponent, strolling calmly along a crosswalk, at the level below.

Dulaq hurried down the next ramp, worked his way through the crowd, and saw the man again. Tall and blond, unmistakable. Dulaq edged along behind him quietly, easily. No disturbance. No pushing. Plenty of time. They walked along the street for a quarter hour while the distance between them slowly shrank from fifty feet to five.

Finally Dulaq was directly behind him, within arm's reach. He grasped the stat-wand and pulled it from his tunic. With one quick motion he touched it to the base of the man's skull and started to thumb the button that would release the killing bolt of energy ...

The man turned suddenly. It wasn't Odal!

Dulaq jerked back in surprise. It couldn't be. He had seen his face. It was Odal—and yet this man was definitely a stranger.

He stared at Dulaq as the duelist backed away a few steps, then turned and walked quickly from the place.

A mistake, Dulaq told himself. *You were overanxious. A good thing this is an hallucination, or else the auto-police would be taking you in by now.*

And yet ... he had been so certain that it was Odal. A chill shuddered through him. He looked up, and there was his antagonist, on the thoroughfare above, at the precise spot where he himself had been a few minutes earlier. Their eyes met, and Odal's lips parted in a cold smile.

Dulaq hurried up the ramp. Odal was gone by the time he reached the upper level. *He could not have gotten far*, Dulaq reasoned. Slowly, but very surely, Dulaq's hallucination turned into a nightmare. He spotted Odal in the crowd, only to have him melt away. He saw him again, lolling in a small park, but when he got closer, the man turned out to be another stranger. He felt the chill of the duelist's ice-blue eyes on him again and again, but when he turned to find his antagonist, no one was there but the impersonal crowd.

Odal's face appeared again and again. Dulaq struggled through the throngs to find his opponent, only to have him vanish. The crowd seemed to be filled with tall, blond men crisscrossing before Dulaq's dismayed eyes.

The shadows lengthened. The sun was setting. Dulaq could feel his heart pounding within him and perspiration pouring from every square inch of his skin.

There he is! Definitely, positively him! Dulaq pushed through the homeward-bound crowds toward the figure of a tall, blond man leaning against the safety railing of the city's main thoroughfare. It was Odal, the damned smiling confident Odal.

Dulaq pulled the wand from his tunic and battled across the surging crowd to the spot where Odal stood motionless, hands in pockets, watching him.

Dulaq came within arm's reach ...

"TIME, GENTLEMEN. TIME IS UP, THE DUEL IS ENDED."

High above the floor of the antiseptic-white chamber that housed the dueling machine was a narrow gallery. Before the machine had been installed, the chamber had been a lecture hall in Acquatainia's largest university. Now the rows of students' seats, the lecturer's dais and rostrum were gone. The chamber held only the machine, the grotesque collection of consoles, control desks, power units, association circuits, and booths where the two antagonists sat.

In the gallery—empty during ordinary duels—sat a privileged handful of newsmen.

"Time limit is up," one of them said. "Dulaq didn't get him."

"Yes, but he didn't get Dulaq, either."

The first one shrugged. "The important thing is that now Dulaq has to fight Odal on his terms. Dulaq couldn't win with his own choice of weapons and situation, so—"

"Wait, they're coming out."

Down on the floor below, Dulaq and his opponent emerged from their enclosed booths.

One of the newsmen whistled softly. "Look at Dulaq's face ... it's positively gray."

"I've never seen the Prime Minister so shaken."

"And take a look at Kanus' hired assassin." The newsmen turned toward Odal, who stood before his booth, quietly chatting with his seconds.

"Hm-m-m. There's a bucket of frozen ammonia for you."

"He's enjoying this."

One of the newsmen stood up. "I've got a deadline to meet. Save my seat."

He made his way past the guarded door, down the rampway circling the outer walls of the building, to the portable tri-di transmitting unit that the Acquatainian government had permitted for the newsmen on the campus grounds outside the former lecture hall.

The newsman huddled with his technicians for a few minutes, then stepped before the transmitter.

"Emile Dulaq, Prime Minister of the Acquataine Cluster and acknowledged leader of the coalition against Chancellor Kanus of the Kerak Worlds, has failed in the first part of his psychonic duel against Major Par Odal of Kerak. The two antagonists are now undergoing the routine medical and psychological checks before renewing their duel."

By the time the newsman returned to his gallery seat, the duel was almost ready to begin again.

Dulaq stood in the midst of a group of advisors before the looming impersonality of the machine.

"You need not go through with the next phase of the duel immediately," his Minister of Defense was saying. "Wait until tomorrow. Rest and calm yourself."

Dulaq's round face puckered into a frown. He cocked an eye at the chief meditech, hovering at the edge of the little group.

The meditech, one of the staff that ran the dueling machine, pointed out, "The Prime Minister has passed the examinations. He is capable, within the agreed-upon rules of the contest, of resuming."

"But he has the option of retiring for the day, does he not?"

"If Major Odal agrees."

Dulaq shook his head impatiently. "No. I shall go through with it. Now."

"But—"

The prime minister's face suddenly hardened; his advisors lapsed into a respectful silence. The chief meditech ushered Dulaq back into his booth. On the other side of the room, Odal glanced at the Acquatainians, grinned humorlessly, and strode to his own booth.

Dulaq sat and tried to blank out his mind while the meditechs adjusted the neurocontacts to his head and torso. They finished at last and withdrew. He was alone in the booth now, looking at the dead-white walls, completely bare except for the viewscreen before his eyes. The screen finally began to glow slightly, then brightened into a series of shifting colors. The colors merged and changed, swirled across his field of view. Dulaq felt himself being drawn into them gradually, compellingly, completely immersed in them.

The mists slowly vanished, and Dulaq found himself standing on an immense and totally barren plain. Not a tree, not a blade of grass; nothing but bare, rocky ground stretching in all directions to the horizon and disturbingly harsh yellow sky. He looked down and at his feet saw the weapon that Odal had chosen.

A primitive club.

With a sense of dread, Dulaq picked up the club and hefted it in his hand. He scanned the plain. Nothing. No hills or trees or bushes to hide in. No place to run to.

And off on the horizon he could see a tall, lithe figure holding a similar club walking slowly and deliberately toward him.

The press gallery was practically empty. The duel had more than an hour to run, and most of the newsmen were outside, broadcasting their hastily-drawn guesses about Dulaq's failure to win with his own choice of weapon and environment.

Then a curious thing happened.

On the master control panel of the dueling machine, a single light flashed red. The meditech blinked at it in surprise, then pressed a series of buttons on his board. More red lights appeared. The chief meditech rushed to the board and flipped a single switch.

One of the newsmen turned to his partner. "What's going on down there?"

"I think it's all over.... Yes, look, they're opening up the booths. Somebody must've scored a victory."

They watched intently while the other newsmen quickly filed back into the gallery.

"There's Odal. He looks happy."

"Guess that means—"

"Good Lord! Look at Dulaq!"

CHAPTER II

Dr. Leoh was lecturing at the Carinae Regional University when the news of Dulaq's duel reached him. An assistant professor perpetrated the unthinkable breach of interrupting the lecture to whisper the news in his ear.

Leoh nodded grimly, hurriedly finished his lecture, and them accompanied the assistant professor to the University president's office. They stood in silence as the slideway whisked them through the strolling students and blossoming greenery of the quietly-busy campus.

Leoh remained wrapped in his thoughts as they entered the administration building and rode the lift tube. Finally, as they stepped through the president's doorway, Leoh asked the assistant professor:

"You say he was in a state of catatonic shock when they removed him from the machine?"

"He still is," the president answered from his desk. "Completely withdrawn from the real world. Cannot speak, hear, or even see—a living vegetable."

Leoh plopped down in the nearest chair and ran a hand across his fleshy face. He was balding and jowly, but his face was creased from a smile that was almost habitual, and his eyes were active and alert.

"I don't understand it," he admitted. "Nothing like this has ever happened in a dueling machine before."

The university president shrugged. "I don't understand it either. But, this is your business." He put a slight emphasis on the last word, unconsciously perhaps.

"Well, at least this will not reflect on the university. That is why I formed Psychonics as a separate business enterprise." Then he added, with a grin, "The money was, of course, only a secondary consideration."

The president managed a smile. "Of course."

"I suppose the Acquatainians want to see me?" Leoh asked academically.

"They're on the tri-di now, waiting for you."

"They're holding a transmission frequency open over eight hundred parsecs?" Leoh looked impressed. "I must be an important man."

"You're the inventor of the dueling machine and the head of Psychonics, Inc. You're the only man who can tell them what went wrong."

"Well, I suppose I shouldn't keep them waiting."

"You can take the call here," the president said, starting to get up from his chair.

"No, no, stay there at your desk," Leoh insisted. "There's no reason for you to leave. Or you either," he said to the assistant professor.

The president touched a button on his desk communicator. The far wall of the office glowed momentarily, then seemed to dissolve. They were looking into another office, this one on Acquatainia. It was crowded with nervous-looking men in business clothes and military uniforms.

"Gentlemen," Dr. Leoh said.

Several of the Acquatainians tried to answer him at once. After a few seconds of talking together, they all looked toward one of their members—a tall, purposeful, shrewd-faced civilian who bore a neatly-trimmed black beard.

"I am Fernd Massan, the Acting Prime Minister of Acquatainia. You realize, of course, the crisis that has been precipitated in my Government because of this duel?"

Leoh blinked. "I realize that apparently there has been some difficulty with the dueling machine installed on the governing planet of your star cluster. Political crises are not in my field."

"But your dueling machine has incapacitated the Prime Minister," one of the generals bellowed.

"And at this particular moment," the defense minister added, "in the midst of our difficulties with the Kerak Worlds."

"If the Prime Minister is not—"

"Gentlemen!" Leoh objected. "I cannot make sense of your story if you all speak at once."

Massan gestured them to silence.

"The dueling machine," Leoh said, adopting a slightly professorial tone, "is nothing more than a psychonic device for alleviating human aggressions and hostilities. It allows for two men to share a dream world created by one of them. There is a nearly-complete feedback between the two. Within certain limits, two men can do anything they wish within their dream world. This allows men to settle grievances with violence—in the safety of their own imaginations. If the machine is operated properly, no physical or mental harm can be done to the participants. They can alleviate their tensions safely—without damage of any sort to anyone, and without hurting society.

"Your own Government tested one of the machines and approved its use on Acquatainia more than three years ago. I see several of you who were among those to whom I personally demonstrated the device. Duelling machines are in use through wide portions of the galaxy, and I am certain that many of you have used the machine. You have, general, I'm sure."

The general blustered. "That has nothing to do with the matter at hand!"

"Admittedly," Leoh conceded. "But I do not understand how a therapeutic machine can possibly become entangled in a political crisis."

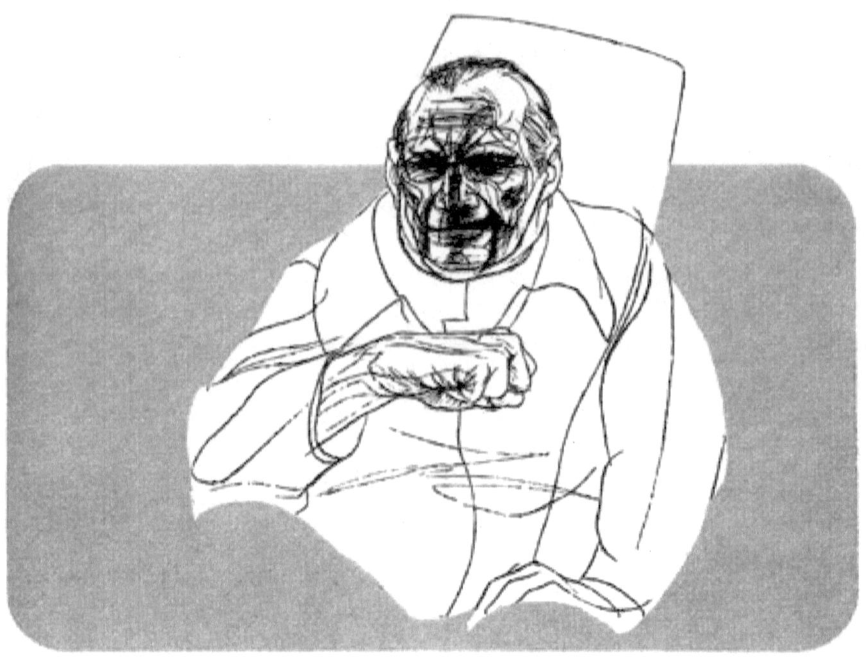

Massan said: "Allow me to explain. Our Government has been conducting extremely delicate negotiations with the stellar governments of our neighboring territories. These negotiations concern the rearmaments of the Kerak Worlds. You have heard of Kanus of Kerak?"

"I recall the name vaguely," Leoh said. "He's a political leader of some sort."

"Of the worst sort. He has acquired complete dictatorship of the Kerak Worlds, and is now attempting to rearm them for war. This is in direct countervention of the Treaty of Acquatainia, signed only thirty Terran years ago."

"I see. The treaty was signed at the end of the Acquataine-Kerak war, wasn't it?"

"A war that we won," the general pointed out.

"And now the Kerak Worlds want to rearm and try again," Leoh said.

"Precisely."

Leoh shrugged. "Why not call in the Star Watch? This is their type of police activity. And what has all this to do with the dueling machine?"

Massan explained patiently, "The Acquataine Cluster has never become a full-fledged member of the Terran Commonwealth. Our neighboring territories are likewise unaffiliated. Therefore the Star Watch can intervene only if all parties concerned agree to intervention. Unless, of course, there is an actual military emergency. The Kerak Worlds, of course, are completely isolationist—unbound by any laws except those of force."

Leoh shook his head.

"As for the dueling machine," Massan went on, "Kanus of Kerak has turned it into a political weapon—"

"But that's impossible. Your government passed strict laws concerning the use of the machine; I recommended them and I was in your Council chambers when the laws were passed. The machine may be used only for personal grievances. It is strictly outside the realm of politics."

Massan shook his head sadly. "Sir, laws are one thing—people are another. And politics consists of people, not words on paper."

"I don't understand," Leoh said.

Massan explained, "A little more than one Terran year ago, Kanus picked a quarrel with a neighboring star-group—the Safad Federation. He wanted an especially favorable trade agreement with them. Their minister of trade objected most strenuously. One of the Kerak negotiators—a certain Major Odal—got into a personal argument with the minister. Before anyone knew what had happened, they had challenged each other to a duel. Odal won the duel, and the minister resigned his post. He said that he could no longer effectively fight against the will of Odal and his group ... he was psychologically incapable of it. Two weeks later he was dead—apparently a suicide, although I have doubts."

"That's ... extremely interesting," Leoh said.

"Three days ago," Massan continued, "the same Major Odal engaged Prime Minister Dulaq in a bitter personal argument. Odal is now a military attaché of the Kerak Embassy here. He accused the Prime Minister of cowardice, before a large group of an Embassy party. The Prime Minister had no alternative but to challenge him. And now—"

"And now Dulaq is in a state of shock, and your government is tottering."

Massan's back stiffened. "Our Government shall not fall, nor shall the Acquataine Cluster acquiesce to the rearmament of the Kerak Worlds. But"—his voice lowered—"without Dulaq, I fear that our neighboring governments will give in to Kanus' demands and allow him to rearm. Alone, we are powerless to stop him."

"Rearmament itself might not be so bad," Leoh mused, "if you can keep the Kerak Worlds from using their weapons. Perhaps the Star Watch might—"

"Kanus could strike a blow and conquer a star system before the Star Watch could be summoned and arrive to stop him. Once Kerak is armed, this entire area of the galaxy is in peril. In fact, the entire galaxy is endangered."

"And he's using the dueling machine to further his ambitions," Leoh said. "Well, gentlemen, it seems I have no alternative but to travel to the Acquataine Cluster. The dueling machine is my responsibility, and if there is something wrong with it, or the use of it, I will do my best to correct the situation."

"That is all we ask," Massan said. "Thank you."

The Acquatainian scene faded away, and the three men in the university president's office found themselves looking at a solid wall once again.

"Well," Dr. Leoh said, turning to the president, "it seems that I must request an indefinite leave of absence."

The president frowned. "And it seems that I must grant your request—even though the year is only half-finished."

"I regret the necessity," Leoh said; then, with a broad grin, he added, "My assistant professor, here, can handle my courses for the remainder of the year very easily. Perhaps he will even be able to deliver his lectures without being interrupted."

The assistant professor turned red.

"Now then," Leoh muttered, mostly to himself, "who is this Kanus, and why is he trying to turn the Kerak Worlds into an arsenal?"

CHAPTER III

Chancellor Kanus, the supreme leader of the Kerak Worlds, stood at the edge of the balcony and looked across the wild, tumbling gorge to the rugged mountains beyond.

"These are the forces that mold men's actions," he said to his small audience of officials and advisors, "the howling winds, the mighty mountains, the open sky and the dark powers of the clouds."

The men nodded and made murmurs of agreement.

"Just as the mountains thrust up from the pettiness of the lands below, so shall we rise above the common walk of men," Kanus said. "Just as a thunderstorm terrifies them, we will make them bend to our will!"

"We will destroy the past," said one of the ministers.

"And avenge the memory of defeat," Kanus added. He turned and looked at the little group of men. Kanus was the smallest man on the balcony: short, spare, sallow-faced; but he possessed piercing dark eyes and a strong voice that commanded attention.

He walked through the knot of men and stopped before a tall, lean, blond youth in light-blue military uniform. "And you, Major Odal, will be a primary instrument in the first steps of conquest."

Odal bowed stiffly. "I only hope to serve my leader and my worlds."

"You shall. And you already have," Kanus said, beaming. "Already the Acquatainians are thrashing about like a snake whose head has been cut off. Without Dulaq, they have no head, no brain to direct them. For your part in this triumph"—Kanus snapped his fingers, and one of his advisors quickly stepped to his side and handed him a small ebony box—"I present you with this token of the esteem of the Kerak Worlds, and of my personal high regard."

He handed the box to Odal, who opened it and took out a small jeweled pin.

"The Star of Kerak," Kanus announced. "This is the first time it has been awarded to anyone except a warrior on the battlefield. But then, we have turned their so-called civilized machine into our own battlefield, eh?"

Odal grinned. "Yes, sir, we have. Thank you very much sir. This is the supreme moment of my life."

"To date, major. Only to date. There will be other moments, even higher ones. Come, let's go inside. We have many plans to discuss ... more duels ... more triumphs."

They all filed in to Kanus' huge, elaborate office. The leader walked across the plushly ornate room and sat at the elevated desk, while his followers arranged themselves in the chairs and couches placed about the floor. Odal remained standing, near the doorway.

Kanus let his fingers flick across a small control board set into his desktop, and a tri-dimensional star map glowed into existence on the far wall. As its center were the eleven stars that harbored the Kerak Worlds. Around them stood neighboring stars, color-coded to show their political groupings. Off to one side of the map was the Acquataine Cluster, a rich mass of stars—wealthy, powerful, the most important political and economic power in the section of the galaxy. Until yesterday's duel.

Kanus began one of his inevitable harangues. Objectives, political and military. Already the Kerak Worlds were unified under his dominant will. The people would follow wherever he led. Already the political alliances built up by the Acquatainian diplomacy since the last war were tottering, now that Dulaq was out of the picture. Now was the time to strike. A political blow *here*, at the Szarno Confederacy, to bring them and their armaments industries into line with Kerak. Then more political strikes to isolate the Acquataine Cluster from its allies, and to build up the subservient states for Kerak. Then, finally, the military blow—against the Acquatainians.

"A sudden strike, a quick, decisive series of blows, and the Acquatainians will collapse like a house of paper. Before the Star Watch can interfere, we will be masters of the Cluster. Then, with the resources of Acquatainia to draw on, we can challenge any force in the galaxy—even the Terran Commonwealth itself!"

The men in the room nodded their assent.

They've heard this story many, many times, Odal thought to himself. This was the first time he had been privileged to listen to it. If you closed your eyes, or looked only at the star map, the plan sounded bizarre, extreme, even impossible. But, if you watched Kanus, and let those piercing, almost hypnotic eyes fasten on yours, then the leader's wildest dreams sounded not only exciting, but inevitable.

Odal leaned a shoulder against the paneled wall and scanned the other men in the room.

There was fat Greber, the vice chancellor, fighting desperately to stay awake after drinking too much wine during the luncheon and afterward. And Modal, sitting on the couch next to him, was bright-eyed and alert, thinking only of how much money and power would come to him as Chief of Industries once the rearmament program began in earnest.

Sitting alone on another couch was Kor, the quiet one, the head of Intelligence, and—technically—Odal's superior. Silent Kor, whose few words were usually charged with terror for those whom he spoke against.

Marshal Lugal looked bored when Kanus spoke of politics, but his face changed when military matters came up. The marshal lived for only one purpose:

to avenge his army's humiliating defeat in the war against the Acquatainians, thirty Terran years ago. What he didn't realize, Odal thought, smiling to himself, was that as soon as he had reorganized the army and re-equipped it, Kanus planned to retire him and place younger men in charge. Men whose only loyalty was not to the army, not even to the Kerak Worlds and their people, but to the chancellor himself.

Eagerly following every syllable, every gesture of the leader was little Tinth. Born to the nobility, trained in the arts, a student of philosophy, Tinth had deserted his heritage and joined the forces of Kanus. His reward had been the Ministry of Education; many teachers had suffered under him.

And finally there was Romis, the Minister of Intergovernmental Affairs. A professional diplomat, and one of the few men in government before Kanus' sweep to power to survive this long. It was clear that Romis hated the chancellor. But he served the Kerak Worlds well. The diplomatic corps was flawless in their handling of intergovernmental affairs. It was only a matter of time, Odal knew, before one of them—Romis or Kanus—killed the other.

The rest of Kanus' audience consisted of political hacks, roughnecks-turned-bodyguards, and a few other hangers-on who had been with Kanus since the days when he held his political monologues in cellars, and haunted the alleys to avoid the police. Kanus had come a long way: from the blackness of oblivion to the dazzling heights of the chancellor's rural estate.

Money, power, glory, revenge, patriotism: each man in the room, listening to Kanus, had his reasons for following the chancellor.

And my reasons? Odal asked himself. *Why do I follow him? Can I see into my own mind as easily as I see into theirs?*

There was duty, of course. Odal was a soldier, and Kanus was the duly-elected leader of the government. Once elected, though, he had dissolved the government and solidified his powers as absolute dictator of the Kerak Worlds.

There was gain to be had by performing well under Kanus. Regardless of his political ambitions and personal tyrannies, Kanus rewarded well when he was pleased. The medal—the Star of Kerak—carried with it an annual pension that would nicely accommodate a family. *If I had one,* Odal thought, sardonically.

There was power, of sorts, also. Working the dueling machine in his special way, hammering a man into nothingness, finding the weaknesses in his personality and exploiting them, pitting his mind against others, turning sneering towers of pride like Dulaq into helpless whipped dogs—that was power. And it was a power that did not go unnoticed in the cities of the Kerak Worlds. Already Odal was easily recognized on the streets; women especially seemed to be attracted to him now.

"The most important factor," Kanus was saying, "and I cannot stress it overmuch, is to build up an aura of invincibility. This is why your work is so important, Major Odal. You must be invincible! Because today you represent the collective will of the Kerak Worlds. To-day you are the instrument of my own will—and you must triumph at every turn. The fate of your people, of your government, of your chancellor rests squarely on your shoulders each time you step into a dueling machine. You have borne that responsibility well, major. Can you carry it even further?"

"I can, sir," Odal answered crisply, "and I will."

Kanus beamed at him. "Good! Because your next duel—and those that follow it—will be to the death."

CHAPTER IV

It took the starship two weeks to make the journey from Carinae to the Acquataine Cluster. Dr. Leoh spent the time checking over the Acquatainian dueling machine, by direct tri-di beam; the Acquatainian government gave him all the technicians, time and money he needed for the task.

Leoh spent as much of his spare time as possible with the other passengers of the ship. He was gregarious, a fine conversationalist, and had a nicely-balanced sense of humor. Particularly, he was a favorite of the younger women, since he had reached the age where he could flatter them with his attention without making them feel endangered.

But still, there were long hours when he was alone in his stateroom with nothing but his memories. At times like these, it was impossible not to think back over the road he had been following.

Albert Robertus Leoh, Ph.D., Professor of Physics, Professor of Electronics, master of computer technology, inventor of the interstellar tri-di communications system; and more recently, student of psychology, Professor of Psychophysiology, founder of Psychonics, Inc., inventor of the dueling machine.

During his earlier years, when the supreme confidence of youth was still with him, Leoh had envisioned himself as helping mankind to spread his colonies and civilizations throughout the galaxy. The bitter years of galactic war had ended in his childhood, and now human societies throughout the Milky Way were linked together—in greater or lesser degree of union—into a more-or-less peaceful coalition of star groups.

There were two great motivating forces at work on those human societies spread across the stars, and these forces worked toward opposite goals. On the one hand was the urge to explore, to reach new stars, new planets, to expand the frontiers of man's civilizations and found new colonies, new nations. Pitted against this drive to expand was an equally-powerful force: the realization that technology had finally put an end to physical labor and almost to poverty itself on all the civilized worlds of man. The urge to move off to the frontier was penned in and buried alive under the enervating comforts of civilization.

The result was inescapable. The civilized worlds became constantly more crowded as time wore on. They became jampacked islands of humanity sprinkled thinly across the sea of space that was still full of unpopulated islands.

The expense and difficulty of interstellar travel was often cited as an excuse. The starships *were* expensive: their power demands were frightful. Only the most determined—and the best financed—groups of colonists could afford them. The rest of mankind accepted the ease and safety of civilization, lived in the bulging cities of the teeming planets. Their lives were circumscribed by their neighbors, and by their governments. Constantly more people crowding into a fixed living space meant constantly less freedom. The freedom to dream, to run free, to procreate, all became state-owned, state-controlled monopolies.

And Leoh had contributed to this situation.

He had contributed his thoughts and his work. He had contributed often and regularly—the interstellar communications systems was only the one outstanding achievement in a long career of achievements.

Leoh had been nearly at the voluntary retirement age for scientists when he realized what he, and his fellow scientists, had done. Their efforts to make life richer and more rewarding for mankind had made life only less strenuous and more rigid.

And with every increase in comfort, Leoh discovered, came a corresponding increase in neuroses, in crimes of violence, in mental aberrations. Senseless wars of pride broke out between star-groups for the first time in generations. Outwardly, the peace of the galaxy was assured; but beneath the glossy surface of the Terran Commonwealth there smoldered the beginnings of a volcano. Police actions fought by the Star Watch were increasing ominously. Petty wars between once-stable peoples were flaring up steadily.

Once Leoh realized the part he had played in this increasingly tragic drama, he was confronted with two emotions—a deep sense of guilt, both personal and professional; and, countering this, a determination to do something, anything, to restore at least some balance to man's collective mentality.

Leoh stepped out of physics and electronics, and entered the field of psychology. Instead of retiring, he applied for a beginner's status in his new profession. It had taken considerable bending and straining of the Commonwealth's rules—but for a man of Leoh's stature, the rules could be flexed somewhat. Leoh became a student once again, then a researcher, and finally a Professor of Psychophysiology.

Out of this came the dueling machine. A combination of electroencephalograph and autocomputer. A dream machine, that amplified a man's imagination until he could engulf himself into a world of his own making.

Leoh envisioned it as a device to enable men to rid themselves of hostility and tension safely. Through his efforts, and those of his colleagues, dueling machines were quickly becoming accepted devices for settling disputes.

When two men had a severe difference of opinion—deep enough to warrant legal action—they could go to the dueling machine instead of the courts. Instead of sitting helplessly and watching the machinations of the law grind impersonally through their differences, the two antagonists could allow their imaginations free rein in the dueling machine. They could settle their differences personally, as violently as they wished, without hurting themselves or anyone else. On most civilized worlds, the results of properly-monitored duels were accepted as legally binding.

The tensions of civilized life could be escaped—albeit temporarily—in the dueling machine. This was a powerful tool, much too powerful to allow it to be used indiscriminately. Therefore Leoh safeguarded his invention by forming a private company—Psychonics, Inc.—and securing an exclusive license from the Terran Commonwealth to manufacture, sell, install and maintain the machines. His customers were government health and legal agencies; his responsibilities were: legally, to the Commonwealth; morally, to all mankind; and finally, to his own restless conscience.

The dueling machines succeeded. They worked as well, and often better, than Leoh had anticipated. But he knew that they were only a stopgap, only a temporarily shoring of a constantly-eroding dam. What was needed, really needed, was some method of exploding the status quo, some means of convincing people to reach out for those unoccupied, unexplored stars that filled the galaxy, some way of convincing men that they should leave the comforts of civilization for the excitement of colonization.

Leoh had been searching for that method when the news of Dulaq's duel against Odal reached him.

Now he was speeding across parsecs of space, praying to himself that the dueling machine had not failed.

The two-week flight ended. The starship took up a parking orbit around the capital planet of Acquataine Cluster. The passengers transhipped to the surface.

Dr. Leoh was met at the landing disk by an official delegation, headed by Massan, the acting prime minister. They exchanged formal greetings there at the base of the ship, while the other passengers hurried by.

As Leoh and Massan, surrounded by the other members of the delegation, rode the slideway to the port's administration building, Leoh commented:

"As you probably know, I have checked through your dueling machine quite thoroughly via tri-di for the past two weeks. I can find nothing wrong with it."

Massan shrugged. "Perhaps you should have checked then, the machine on Szarno."

"The Szarno Confederation? Their dueling machine?"

"Yes. This morning Kanus' hired assassin killed a man in it."

"He won another duel," Leoh said.

"You do not understand," Massan said grimly, "Major Odal's opponent—an industrialist who had spoken out against Kanus—was actually killed in the dueling machine. The man is dead!"

CHAPTER V

One of the advantages of being Commander-in-Chief of the Star Watch, the old man thought to himself, is that you can visit any planet is the Commonwealth.

He stood at the top of the hill and looked out over the green table land of Kenya. This was the land of his birth, Earth was his homeworld. The Star Watch's official headquarters may be in the heart of a globular cluster of stars near the center of the galaxy, but Earth was the place the commander wanted most to see as he grew older and wearier.

An aide, who had been following the commander at a respectful distance, suddenly intruded himself in the old man's reverie.

"Sir, a message for you."

The commander scowled at the young officer. "I gave orders that I was not to be disturbed."

The officer, slim and stiff in his black-and-silver uniform, replied. "Your chief of staff has passed the message on to you, sir. It's from Dr. Leoh, of Carinae University. Personal and urgent, sir."

The old man grumbled to himself, but nodded. The aide placed a small crystalline sphere on the grass before him. The air above the sphere started to vibrate and glow.

"Sir Harold Spencer here," the commander said.

The bubbling air seemed to draw in on itself and take solid form. Dr. Leoh sat at a desk chair and looked up at the standing commander.

"Harold, it's a pleasure to see you once again."

Spencer's stern eyes softened, and his beefy face broke into a well-creased smile. "Albert, you ancient scoundrel. What do you mean by interrupting my first visit home in fifteen years?"

"It won't be a long interruption," Leoh said.

"You told my chief of staff that it was urgent," Sir Harold groused.

"It is. But it's not the sort of problem that requires much action on your part. Yet. You are familiar with recent political developments on the Kerak Worlds?"

Spencer snorted. "I know that a barbarian named Kanus has established himself as a dictator. He's a troublemaker. I've been talking to the Commonwealth Council about the advisability of quashing him before he causes grief, but you know the Council ... first wait until the flames have sprung up, then thrash about and demand that the Star Watch do something!"

Leoh grinned. "You're as irascible as ever."

"My personality is not the subject of this rather expensive discussion. What about Kanus? And what are you doing, getting yourself involved in politics? About to change your profession again?"

"No, not at all," Leoh answered, laughing. Then, more seriously. "It seems as though Kanus has discovered some method of using the dueling machines to achieve political advantages over his neighbors."

"What?"

Leoh explained the circumstances of Odal's duels with the Acquatainian prime minister and Szarno Industrialist.

"Dulaq is completely incapacitated and the other poor fellow is dead?" Spencer's face darkened into a thundercloud. "You were right to call me. This is a situation that could easily become intolerable."

"I agree," Leoh said. "But evidently Kanus has not broken any laws or interstellar agreements. All that meets the eye is a disturbing pair of accidents, both of them accruing to Kanus' benefit."

"Do you believe that they were accidents?"

"Certainly not. The dueling machine cannot cause physical or mental harm ... unless someone has tampered with it in some way."

"That is my thought, too." Spencer was silent for a moment, weighing the matter in his mind. "Very well. The Star Watch cannot act officially, but there is nothing to prevent me from dispatching an officer to the Acquataine Cluster, on detached duty, to serve as liaison between us."

"Good. I think that will be the most effective method of handling the situation, at present."

"It will be done." Sir Harold pronounced. His aide made a mental note of it.

"Thank you very much," Leoh said. "Now, go back to enjoying your vacation."

"Vacation? This is no vacation," Spencer rumbled. "I happen to be celebrating my birthday."

"So? Well, congratulations. I try not to remember mine," Leoh said.

"Then you must be older than I," Spencer replied, allowing only the faintest hint of a smile to appear.

"I suppose it's possible."

"But not very likely, eh?"

They laughed together and said good-by. The Star Watch commander tramped through the hills until sunset, enjoying the sight of the grasslands and distant purple mountains he had known in his childhood. As dusk closed in, he told his aide he was ready to leave.

The aide pressed a stud on his belt and a two-place aircar skimmed silently from the far side of the hills and hovered beside them. Spencer climbed in laboriously while the aide remained discreetly at his side. While the commander settled his bulk into his seat the aide hurried around the car and hopped into his place. The car glided off toward Spencer's personal planetship, waiting for him at a nearby field.

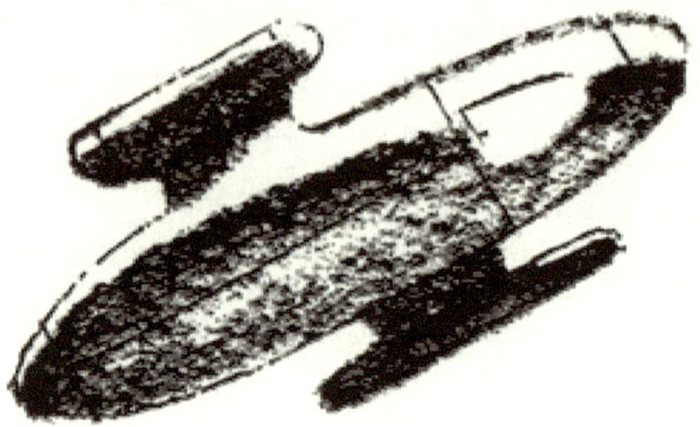

"Don't forget to assign an officer to Dr. Leoh," the commander muttered to his aide. Then he turned and watched the unmatchable beauty of an Earthly sunset.

The aide did not forget the assignment. That night, as Sir Harold's ship spiraled out to a rendezvous with a starship, the aide dictated the necessary order into a autodispatcher that immediately beamed it to the Star Watch's nearest communications center, on Mars.

The order was scanned and routed automatically and finally beamed to the Star Watch unit commandant in charge of the area closest to the Acquataine Cluster, on the sixth planet circling the star Perseus Alpha. Here again, the order was processed automatically and routed through the local headquarters to the personnel files. The automated files selected three microcard dossiers that matched the requirements of the order.

The three microcards and the order itself appeared simultaneously on the desktop viewer of the Star Watch personnel officer. He looked at the order, then read the dossiers. He flicked a button that gave him an updated status report on each of the three men in question. One was due for leave after an extensive period of duty. The second was the son of a personal friend of the local commandant. The third had just arrived a few weeks ago, fresh from the Star Watch Academy on Mars.

The personnel officer selected the third man, routed his dossier and Sir Harold's order back into the automatic processing system, and returned to the film of primitive dancing girls he had been watching before this matter of decision had arrived at his desk.

CHAPTER VI

The space station orbiting around Acquatainia—the capital planet of the Acquataine Cluster—served simultaneously as a transfer point from starships to planetships, a tourist resort, meteorological station, communications center, scientific laboratory, astronomical observatory, medical haven for allergy and cardiac patients, and military base. It was, in reality, a good-sized city with its own markets, its own local government, and its own way of life.

Dr. Leoh had just stepped off the debarking ramp of the starship from Szarno. The trip there had been pointless and fruitless. But he had gone anyway, in the slim hope that he might find something wrong with the dueling machine that had been used to murder a man.

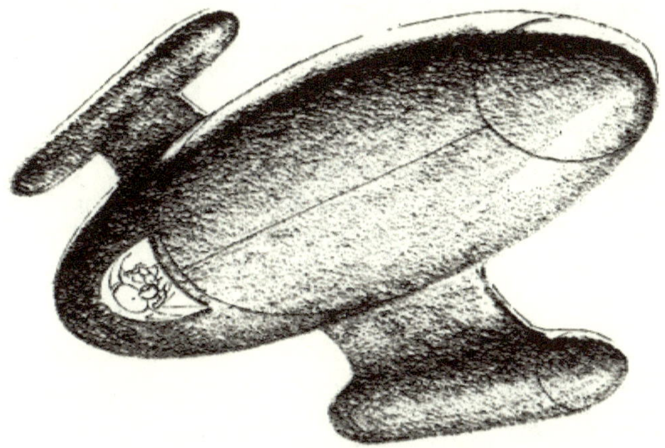

A shudder went through him as he edged along the automated customs scanners and paper-checkers. What kind of people could these men of Kerak be? To actually kill a human being in cold blood; to plot and plan the death of a fellow man. Worse than barbaric. Savage.

He felt tired as he left customs and took the slideway to the planetary shuttle ships. Halfway there, he decided to check at the communications desk for messages. That Star Watch officer that Sir Harold had promised him a week ago should have arrived by now.

The communications desk consisted of a small booth that contained the output printer of a communications computer and an attractive young dark-haired girl. Automation or not, Leoh thought smilingly, there were certain human values that transcended mere efficiency.

A lanky, thin-faced youth was half-leaning on the booth's counter, trying to talk to the girl. He had curly blond hair and crystal blue eyes; his clothes consisted of an ill-fitting pair of slacks and tunic. A small traveler's kit rested on the floor at his feet.

"So, I was sort of, well, thinking ... maybe somebody might, uh, show me around ... a little," he was stammering to the girl. "I've never been, uh, here ..."

"It's the most beautiful planet in the galaxy," the girl was saying. "Its cities are the finest."

"Yes ... well, I was sort of thinking ... that is, I know we just, uh, met a few minutes ago ... but, well, maybe ... if you have a free day or so coming up ... maybe we could, uh, sort of—".

She smiled coolly. "I have two days off at the end of the week, but I'll be staying here at the station. There's so much to see and do here, I very seldom leave."

"Oh—"

"You're making a mistake," Leoh interjected dogmatically, "If you have such a beautiful planet for your homeworld, why in the name of the gods of intellect don't you go down there and enjoy it? I'll wager you haven't been out in the natural beauty and fine cities you spoke of since you started working here on the station."

"Why, you're right," she said, surprised.

"You see? You youngsters are all alike. You never think further than the ends of your noses. You should return to the planet, young lady, and see the sunshine again. Why don't you visit the University at the capital city? Plenty of open space and greenery, lots of sunshine and available young men!"

Leoh was grinning broadly, and the girl smiled back at him. "Perhaps I will," she said.

"Ask for me when you get to the University. I'm Dr. Leoh. I'll see to it that you're introduced to some of the girls and gentlemen of your own age."

"Why ... thank you, doctor. I'll do it this week end."

"Good. Now then, any messages for me? Anyone aboard the station looking for me?"

The girl turned and tapped a few keys on the computer's console. A row of lights flicked briefly across the console's face. She turned back to Leoh:

"No, sir, I'm sorry. No message and no one has asked for you."

"Hm-m-m. That's strange. Well, thank you ... and I'll expect to see you at the end of this week."

The girl smiled a farewell. Leoh started to walk away from the booth, back toward the slideway. The young man took a step toward him, stumbled on his own traveling kit, and staggered across the floor for a half-dozen steps before regaining his balance. Leoh turned and saw that the youth's face bore a somewhat ridiculous expression of mixed indecision and curiosity.

"Can I help you?" Leoh asked, stopping at the edge of the moving slideway.

"How ... how did you do that, sir?"

"Do what?"

"Get that girl to agree to visit the university. I've been talking to her for half an hour, and, well, she wouldn't even look straight at me."

Leoh broke into a chuckle. "Well, young man, to begin with, you were much too flustered. It made you appear overanxious. On the other hand, I am at an age where I can be strictly platonic. She was on guard against you, but she knows she has very little to fear from me."

"I see ... I think."

"Well," Leoh said, gesturing toward the slideway, "I suppose this is where we go our separate ways."

"Oh, no, sir. I'm going with you. That is, I mean, you *are* Dr. Leoh, aren't you?"

"Yes, I am. And you must be—" Leoh hesitated. *Can this be a Star Watch officer?* he wondered.

The youth stiffened to attention and for an absurd flash of a second, Leoh thought he was going to salute. "I am Junior Lieutenant Hector, sir; on special detached duty from the cruiser SW4-J188, home base Perseus Alpha VI."

"I see," Leoh replied. "Um-m-m ... is Hector your first name or your last?"

"Both, sir."

I should have guessed, Leoh told himself. Aloud, he said, "Well, lieutenant, we'd better get to the shuttle before it leaves without us."

They took to the slideway. Half a second later, Hector jumped off and dashed back to the communications desk for his traveling kit. He hurried back to Leoh bumping into seven bewildered citizens of various descriptions and nearly breaking both his legs when he tripped as he ran back onto the moving slideway. He went down on his face, sprawled across two lanes moving at different speeds, and needed the assistance of several persons before he was again on his feet and standing beside Leoh.

"I ... I'm sorry to cause all that, uh, commotion, sir."

"That's all right. You weren't hurt, were you?"

"Uh, no ... I don't think so. Just embarrassed."

Leoh said nothing. They rode the slideway in silence through the busy station and out to the enclosed berths where the planetary shuttles were docked. They boarded one of the ships and found a pair of seats.

"Just how long have you been with Star Watch, lieutenant?"

"Six weeks, sir. Three weeks aboard a starship bringing me out to Perseus

Alpha VI, a week at the planetary base there, and two weeks aboard the cruiser SW4-J188. That is, it's been six weeks since I received my commission. I've been at the Academy ... the Star Watch Academy on Mars ... for four years."

"You got through the Academy in four years?"

"That's the regulation time, sir."

"Yes, I know."

The ship eased out of its berth. There was a moment of free-fall, then the drive engine came on and the grav-field equilibrated.

"Tell me, lieutenant, how did you get picked for this assignment?"

"I wish I knew, sir," Hector said, his lean face twisting into a puzzled frown. "I was working out a program for the navigation officer ... aboard the cruiser. I'm pretty good at that ... I can work out computer programs in my head, mostly. Mathematics was my best subject at the Academy —"

"Interesting."

"Yes, well, anyway, I was working out this program when the captain himself came on deck and started shaking my hand telling me that I was being sent on special duty on Acquatainia by direct orders of the Commander-in-Chief. He seemed very happy ... the captain, that is."

"He was no doubt pleased to see you get such an unusual assignment," Leoh said tactfully.

"I'm not sure," Hector said truthfully. "I think he regarded me as some sort of a problem, sir. He had me on a different duty-berth practically every day I was on board the ship."

"Well now," Leoh changed the subject, "what do you know about psychonics?"

"About what, sir?"

"Eh ... electroencephalography?"

Hector looked blank.

"Psychology, perhaps?" Leoh suggested, hopefully, "Physiology? Computer molectronics?"

"I'm pretty good at mathematics!"

"Yes, I know. Did you, by any chance, receive any training in diplomatic affairs?"

"At the Star Watch Academy? No, sir."

Leah ran a hand through his thinning hair. "Then why did the Star Watch select you for this job? I must confess, lieutenant, that I can't understand the workings of a military organization."

Hector shook his head ruefully, "Neither do I, sir."

CHAPTER VII

The next week was an enervatingly slow one for Leoh, evenly divided between tedious checking of each component of the dueling machine, and shameless ruses to keep Hector as far away from the machine as possible.

The Star Watchman certainly wanted to help, and he actually was little short of brilliant in doing intricate mathematics completely in his head. But he was, Leoh found, a clumsy, chattering, whistling, scatterbrained, inexperienced bundle of noise and nerves. It was impossible to do constructive work with him nearby.

Perhaps you're judging him too harshly, Leoh warned himself. *You just might be letting your frustrations with the dueling machine get the better of your sense of balance.*

The professor was sitting in the office that the Acquatainians had given him in one end of the former lecture hall that held the dueling machine. Leoh could see its impassive metal hulk through the open office door.

The room he was sitting in had been one of a suite of offices used by the permanent staff of the machine. But they had moved out of the building completely, in deference to Leoh, and the Acquatainian government had turned the other cubbyhole offices into sleeping rooms for the professor and the Star Watchman, and an auto-kitchen. A combination cook-valet-handyman appeared twice each day—morning and evening—to handle any special chores that the cleaning machines and auto-kitchen might miss.

Leoh slouched back in his desk chair and cast a weary eye on the stack of papers that recorded the latest performances of the machine. Earlier that day he had taken the electroencephalographic records of clinical cases of catatonia and run them through the machine's input unit. The machine immediately rejected them, refused to process them through the amplification units and association circuits.

In other words, the machine had recognized the EEG traces as something harmful to a human being.

Then how did it happen to Dulaq? Leoh asked himself for the thousandth time. It couldn't have been the machine's fault; it must have been something in Odal's mind that simply overpowered Dulaq's.

"Overpowered?" That's a terribly unscientific term, Leoh argued against himself.

Before he could carry the debate any further, he heard the main door of the big chamber slide open and then bang shut, and Hector's off-key whistle shrilled and echoed through the high-vaulted room.

Leoh sighed and put his self-contained argument off to the back of his mind.

Trying to think logically near Hector was a hopeless prospect.

"Are you in, doctor?" Hector's voice rang out.

"In here."

Hector ducked in through the doorway and plopped his rangy frame on the office's couch.

"Everything going well, sir?"

Leoh shrugged. "Not very well, I'm afraid. I can't find anything wrong with the dueling machine. I can't even *force* it to malfunction."

"Well, that's good, isn't it?" Hector chirped happily.

"In a sense," Leoh admitted, feeling slightly nettled at the youth's boundless, pointless optimism. "But, you see, it means that Kanus' people can do things with the machine that I can't."

Hector frowned, considering the problem. "Hm-m-m ... yes, I guess that's right, too, isn't it?"

"Did you see the girl back to her ship safely?" Leoh asked.

"Yes, sir," Hector replied, bobbing his head vigorously. "She's on her way back to the communications booth at the space station. She said to tell you she enjoyed her visit very much."

"Good. It was, eh, very good of you to escort her about the campus. It kept her out of my hair ... what's left of it, that is."

Hector grinned. "Oh, I liked showing her around, and all that—And, well, it sort of kept me out of your hair, too, didn't it?"

Leoh's eyebrows shot up in surprise.

Hector laughed. "Doctor, I may be clumsy, and I'm certainly no scientist ... but I'm not completely brainless."

"I'm sorry if I gave you that impression—"

"Oh no ... don't be sorry. I didn't mean that to sound so ... well, the way it sounded ... that is. I know I'm just in your way—" He started to get up.

Leoh waved him back to the couch. "Relax, my boy, relax. You know, I've been sitting here all afternoon wondering what to do next. Somehow, just now, I came to a conclusion."

"Yes?"

"I'm going to leave the Acquataine Cluster and return to Carinae."

"What? But you can't! I mean—"

"Why not? I'm not accomplishing anything here. Whatever it is that this Odal and Kanus have been doing, it's basically a political problem, and not a scientific one. The professional staff of the machine here will catch up to their tricks sooner or later."

"But, sir, if you can't find the answer, how can they?"

"Frankly, I don't know. But, as I said, this is a political problem more than a scientific one. I'm tired and frustrated and I'm feeling my years. I want to return to Carinae and spend the next few months considering beautifully abstract problems about instantaneous transportation devices. Let Massan and the Star Watch worry about Kanus."

"Oh! That's what I came to tell you. Massan has been challenged to a duel by Odal!"

"What?"

"This afternoon, Odal went to the Council building. Picked an argument with Massan right in the main corridor and challenged him."

"Massan accepted?" Leoh asked.

Hector nodded.

Leoh leaned across his desk and reached for the phone unit. It took a few minutes and a few levels of secretaries and assistants, but finally Massan's dark, bearded face appeared on the screen above the desk.

"You have accepted Odal's challenge?" Leoh asked, without preliminaries.

"We meet next week," Massan replied gravely.

"You should have refused."

"On what pretext?"

"No pretext. A flat refusal, based on the certainty that Odal or someone else from Kerak is tampering with the dueling machine."

Massan shook his head sadly. "My dear learned sir, you still do not comprehend the political situation. The Government of the Acquataine Cluster is much closer to dissolution than I dare to admit openly. The coalition of star groups that Dulaq had constructed to keep the Kerak Worlds neutralized has broken apart completely. This morning, Kanus announced that he would annex Szarno. This afternoon, Odal challenges me."

"I think I see—"

"Of course. The Acquatainian Government is paralyzed now, until the outcome of the duel is known. We cannot effectively intervene in the Szarno crisis until we know who will be heading the Government next week. And, frankly, more than a few members of our Council are now openly favouring Kanus and urging that we establish friendly relations with him before it is too late."

"But, that's all the more reason for refusing the duel," Leoh insisted.

"And be accused of cowardice in my own Council meetings?" Massan smiled grimly. "In politics, my dear sir, the *appearance* of a man means much more than his substance. As a coward, I would soon be out of office. But perhaps, as the winner of a duel against the invincible Odal ... or even as a martyr ... I may accomplish something useful."

Leoh said nothing.

Massan continued, "I put off the duel for a week, hoping that in that time you might discover Odal's secret. I dare not postpone the duel any longer; as it is, the political situation may collapse about our heads at any moment."

"I'll take this machine apart and rebuild it again, molecule by molecule," Leoh promised.

As Massan's image faded from the screen, Leoh turned to Hector. "We have one week to save his life."

"And avert a war, maybe," Hector added.

"Yes." Leoh leaned back in his chair and stared off into infinity.

Hector shuffled his feet, rubbed his nose, whistled a few bars of off-key tunes, and finally blurted, "How can you take apart the dueling machine?"

"Hm-m-m?" Leoh snapped out of his reverie.

"How can you take apart the dueling machine?" Hector repeated. "Looks like a big job to do in a week."

"Yes, it is. But, my boy, perhaps we ... the two of us ... can do it."

Hector scratched his head. "Well, uh, sir ... I'm not very ... that is, my mechanical aptitude scores at the Academy—"

Leoh smiled at him. "No need for mechanical aptitude, my boy. You were trained to fight, weren't you? We can do the job mentally."

CHAPTER VIII

It was the strangest week of their lives.

Leoh's plan was straightforward: to test the dueling machine, push it to the limits of its performance, by actually operating it—by fighting duels.

They started off easily enough, tentatively probing and flexing their mental muscles. Leoh had used the dueling machine himself many times in the past, but only in tests of the machines' routine performance. Never in actual combat against another human being. To Hector, of course, the machine was a totally new and different experience.

The Acquatainian staff plunged into the project without question, providing Leoh with invaluable help in monitoring and analyzing the duels.

At first, Leoh and Hector did nothing more than play hide-and-seek, with one of them picking an environment and the other trying to find his opponent in it. They wandered through jungles and cities, over glaciers and interplanetary voids, seeking each other—without ever leaving the booths of the dueling machine.

Then, when Leoh was satisfied that the machine could reproduce and amplify thought patterns with strict fidelity, they began to fight light duels. The fenced with blunted foils—Hector won, of course, because of his much faster reflexes. Then they tried other weapons—pistols, sonic beams, grenades—but always wearing protective equipment. Strangely, even though Hector was trained in the use of these weapons, Leoh won almost all the bouts. He was neither faster nor more accurate, when they were target-shooting. But when the two of them faced each other, somehow Leoh almost always won.

The machine project more than thoughts, Leoh told himself. *It projects personality.*

They worked in the dueling machine day and night now, enclosed in the booths for twelve or more hours a day, driving themselves and the machine's regular staff to near-exhaustion. When they gulped their meals, between duels, they were physically ragged and sharp-tempered. They usually fell asleep in Leoh's office, while discussing the results of the day's work.

The duels grew slowly more serious. Leoh was pushing the machine to its limits now, carefully extending the rigors of each bout. And yet, even though he knew exactly what and how much he intended to do in each fight, it often took a conscious effort of will to remind himself that the battles he was fighting were actually imaginary.

As the duels became more dangerous, and the artificially-amplified hallucinations began to end in blood and death, Leoh found himself winning more and more frequently. With one part of his mind he was driving to analyze the cause of his consistent success. But another part of him was beginning to really enjoy his prowess.

The strain was telling on Hector. The physical exertion of constant work and practically no relief was considerable in itself. But the emotional effects of being "hurt" and "killed" repeatedly were infinitely worse.

"Perhaps we should stop for a while," Leoh suggested after the fourth day of tests.

"No, I'm all right."

Leoh looked at him. Hector's face was haggard, his eyes bleary.

"You've had enough," Leoh said quietly.

"Please don't make me stop," Hector begged. "I ... I can't stop now. Please give me a chance to do better. I'm improving ... I lasted twice as long in this afternoon's two duels as I did in the ones this morning. Please, don't end it now ... not while I'm completely lost—"

Leoh stared at him, "You want to go on?"

"Yes, sir."

"And if I say no?"

Hector hesitated. Leoh sensed he was struggling with himself. "If you say no," he answered dully, "then it will be no. I can't argue against you any more."

Leoh was silent for a long moment. Finally he opened a desk drawer and took a small bottle from it. "Here, take a sleep capsule. When you wake up we'll try again."

It was dawn when they began again. Leoh entered the dueling machine determined to allow Hector to win. He gave the youthful Star Watchman his choice of weapon and environment. Hector picked one-man scoutships, in planetary orbits. Their weapons were conventional force beams.

But despite his own conscious desire, Leoh found himself winning! The ships spiraled about an unnamed planet, their paths intersecting at least once in every orbit. The problem was to estimate your opponent's orbital position, and then program your own ship so that you arrived at that position either behind or to one side of him. Then you could train your guns on him before he could turn on you.

The problem should have been an easy one for Hector, with his knack for intuitive mental calculation. But Leoh scored the first hit—Hector had piloted his ship into an excellent firing position, but his shot went wide; Leoh maneuvered around clumsily, but managed to register an inconsequential hit on the side of Hector's ship.

In the next three passes, Leoh scored two more hits. Hector's ship was badly damaged now. In return, the Star Watchman had landed one glancing shot on Leoh's ship.

They came around again, and once more Leoh had outguessed his younger opponent. He trained his guns on Hector's ship, then hesitated with his hand poised above the firing button.

Don't kill him again, he warned himself. *His mind can't accept another defeat.*

But Leoh's hand, almost of its own will, reached the button and touched it lightly. Another gram of pressure and the guns would fire.

In that instant's hesitation. Hector pulled his crippled ship around and aimed at Leoh. The Watchman fired a searing blast that jarred Leoh's ship from end to end. Leoh's hand slammed down on the firing button, whether he intended to do it or not, he did not know.

Leoh's shot raked Hector's ship but did not stop it. The two vehicles were hurtling directly at each other. Leoh tried desperately to avert a collision, but Hector bored in grimly, matching Leoh's maneuvers with his own.

The two ships smashed together and exploded.

Abruptly, Leoh found himself in the cramped booth of the dueling machine, his body cold and damp with perspiration, his hands trembling.

He squeezed out of the booth and took a deep breath. Warm sunlight was streaming into the high-vaulted room. The white walls glared brilliantly. Through the tall windows he could see trees and people and clouds in the sky.

Hector walked up to him. For the first time in several days, the Watchman was smiling. Not much, but smiling. "Well, we broke even on that one."

Leoh smiled back, somewhat shakily. "Yes. It was ... quite an experience. I've never died before."

Hector fidgeted, "It's uh, not so bad, I guess—It does sort of, well, shatter you, you know."

"Yes I can see that now."

"Another duel?" Hector asked, nodding his head toward the machine.

"Let's get out of this place for a few hours. Are you hungry?"

"Starved."

They fought seven more duels over the next day and a half. Hector won three of them. It was late afternoon when Leoh called a halt to the tests.

"We can still get in another one or two," the Watchman pointed out.

"No need," Leoh said. "I have all the data I require. Tomorrow Massan meets Odal, unless we can put a stop to it. We have much to do before tomorrow morning."

Hector sagged into the couch. "Just as well. I think I've aged seven years in the past seven days."

"No, my boy," Leoh said gently. "You haven't aged. You've matured."

CHAPTER IX

It was deep twilight when the groundcar slid to a halt on its cushions of compressed air before the Kerak Embassy.

"I still think it's a mistake to go in there." Hector said. "I mean, you could've called him on the tri-di just as well, couldn't you?"

Leoh shook his head. "Never give an agency of any government the opportunity to say 'hold the line a moment' and then huddle together to consider what to do with you. Nineteen times out of twenty, they'll end by passing your request up to the next higher echelon, and you'll be left waiting for weeks."

"Still," Hector insisted, "you're simply stepping into enemy territory. It's a chance you shouldn't take."

"They wouldn't dare touch us."

Hector did not reply, but he looked unconvinced.

"Look," Leoh said, "there are only two men alive who can shed light on this matter. One of them is Dulaq, and his mind is closed to us for an indefinite time, Odal is the only other one who knows what happened."

Hector shook his head skeptically. Leoh shrugged, and opened the door of the groundcar. Hector had no choice but to get out and follow him as he walked up the pathway to the main entrance of the Embassy. The building stood gaunt and gray in the dusk, surrounded by a precisely-clipped hedge. The entrance was flanked by a pair of tall evergreen trees.

Leoh and Hector were met just inside the entrance by a female receptionist. She looked just a trifle disheveled—as though she had been rushed to the desk at a moment's notice. They asked for Odal, were ushered into a sitting room, and within a few minutes—to Hector's surprise—were informed by the girl that Major Odal would be with them shortly.

"You see," Leoh pointed out jovially, "when you come in person they haven't as much of a chance to consider how to get rid of you."

Hector glanced around the windowless room and contemplated the thick, solidly closed door. "There's a lot of scurrying going on on the other side of that door, I'll bet. I mean ... they may be considering how to, uh, get rid of us ... permanently."

Leoh shook his head, smiling wryly. "Undoubtedly the approach closest to their hearts—but highly improbable in the present situation. They have been making most efficient and effective use of the dueling machine to gain their ends."

Odal picked this moment to open the door.

"Dr. Leoh ... Lt. Hector ... you asked to see me?"

"Thank you, Major Odal; I hope you will be able to help me," Leoh said. "You are the only man living who may be able to give us some clues to the failure of the Dueling Machine."

Odal's answering smile reminded Leoh of the best efforts of the robot-puppet designers to make a machine that smiled like a man. "I am afraid I can be of no assistance, Dr. Leoh. My experiences in the machine are ... private."

"Perhaps you don't fully understand the situation," Leoh said. "In the past week, we have tested the dueling machine here on Acquatainia exhaustively. We have learned that its performance can be greatly influenced by a man's personality, and by training. You have fought many duels in the machines. Your background of experience, both as a professional soldier and in the machines, gives you a decided advantage over your opponents.

"However, even with all this considered, I am convinced that you cannot kill a man in the machine—under normal circumstances. We have demonstrated that fact in our tests. An unsabotaged machine cannot cause actual physical harm.

"Yet you have already killed one man and incapacitated another. Where will it stop?"

Odal's face remained calm, except for the faintest glitter of fire deep in his eyes. His voice was quiet, but had the edge of a well-honed blade to it: "I cannot be blamed for my background and experience. And I have not tampered with your machines."

The door to the room opened, and a short, thick-set, bullet-headed man entered. He was dressed in a dark street suit, so that it was impossible to guess his station at the Embassy.

"Would the gentlemen care for refreshments?" he asked in a low-pitched voice.

"No, thank you," Leoh said.

"Some Kerak wine, perhaps?"

"Well—"

"I don't, uh, think we'd better, sir," Hector said. "Thanks all the same."

The man shrugged and sat at a chair next to the door.

Odal turned back to Leoh. "Sir, I have my duty. Massan and I duel tomorrow. There is no possibility of postponing it."

"Very well," Leoh said. "Will you at least allow us to place some special instrumentation into the booth with you, so that we can monitor the duel more fully? We can do the same with Massan. I know the duels are normally private and you would be within your legal rights to refuse the request. But, morally—"

The smile returned to Odal's face. "You wish to monitor my thoughts. To record them and see how I perform during the duel. Interesting. Very interesting—"

The man at the door rose and said, "If you have no desire for refreshments, gentlemen—"

Odal turned to him. "Thank you for your attention."

Their eyes met and locked for an instant. The man give a barely perceptible shake of his head, then left.

Odal returned his attention to Leoh, "I am sorry, professor, but I cannot allow you to monitor my thoughts during the duel."

"But—"

"I regret having to refuse you. But, as you yourself pointed out, there is no legal requirement for such a course of action. I must refuse. I hope you understand."

Leoh rose from the couch, and Hector popped up beside him. "I'm afraid I do understand. And I, too, regret your decision."

Odal escorted them out to their car. They drove away, and the Kerak major walked slowly back into the Embassy building. He was met in the hallway by the dark-suited man who had sat in on the conversation.

"I could have let them monitor my thoughts and still crush Massan," Odal said. "It would have been a good joke on them."

The man grunted. "I have just spoken to the Chancellor on the tri-di, and obtained permission to make a slight adjustment in our plans."

"An adjustment, Minister Kor?"

"After your duel tomorrow, your next opponent will be the eminent Dr. Leoh," Kor said.

CHAPTER X

The mists swirled deep and impenetrable about Fernd Massan. He stared blindly through the useless viewplate in his helmet, then reached up slowly and carefully to place the infrared detector before his eyes.

I never realized an hallucination could seem so real, Massan thought.

Since the challenge by Odal, he realized, the actual world had seemed quite unreal. For a week, he had gone through the motions of life, but felt as though he were standing aside, a spectator mind watching its own body from a distance. The gathering of his friends and associates last night, the night before the duel—that silent, funereal group of people—it had seemed completely unreal to him.

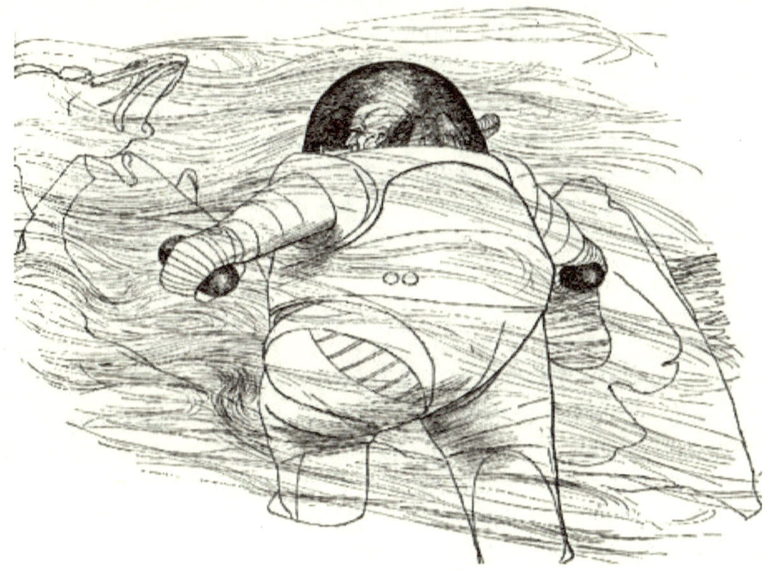

But now, in this manufactured dream, he seemed vibrantly alive. Every sensation was solid, stimulating. He could feel his pulse throbbing through him. Somewhere out in those mists, he knew, was Odal. And the thought of coming to grips with the assassin filled him with a strange satisfaction.

Massan had spent a good many years serving his government on the rich but inhospitable high-gravity planets of the Acquataine Cluster. This was the environment he had chosen: crushing gravity; killing pressures; atmosphere of ammonia and hydrogen, laced with free radicals of sulphur and other valuable but deadly chemicals; oceans of liquid methane and ammonia; "solid ground" consisting of quickly crumbling, eroding ice; howling superpowerful winds that could pick up a mountain of ice and hurl it halfway around the planet; darkness; danger; death.

He was encased in a one-man protective outfit that was half armored suit, half vehicle. There was an internal grav field to keep him comfortable in 3.7 gees, but still the suit was cumbersome, and a man could move only very slowly in it, even with the aid of servomotors.

The weapon he had chosen was simplicity itself—a hand-sized capsule of oxygen. But in a hydrogen/ammonia atmosphere, oxygen could be a deadly explosive. Massan carried several of these "bombs"; so did Odal. *But the trick,* Massan thought to himself, *is to know how to throw them under these conditions; the proper range, the proper trajectory. Not an easy thing to learn, without years of experience.*

The terms of the duel were simple: Massan and Odal were situated on a rough-topped iceberg that was being swirled along one of the methane/ammonia ocean's vicious currents. The ice was rapidly crumbling; the duel would end when the iceberg was completely broken up.

Massan edged along the ragged terrain. His suit's grippers and rollers automatically adjusted to the roughness of the topography. He concentrated his attention on the infrared detector that hung before his viewplate.

A chunk of ice the size of a man's head sailed through the murky atmosphere in a steep glide peculiar to heavy gravity and banged into the shoulder of Massan's suit. The force was enough to rock him slightly off-balance before the servos readjusted. Massan withdrew his arm from the sleeve and felt the inside of the shoulder seam. *Dented, but not penetrated.* A leak would have been disastrous, possibly fatal. Then he remembered: *Of course—I cannot be killed except by direct action of my antagonist. That is one of the rules of the game.*

Still, he carefully fingered the dented shoulder to make certain it was not leaking. The dueling machine and its rules seemed so very remote and unsubstantial, compared to this freezing, howling inferno.

He diligently set about combing the iceberg, determined to find Odal and kill him before their floating island disintegrated. He thoroughly explored every projection, every crevice, every slope, working his way slowly from one end of the 'berg toward the other. Back and forth, cross and re-cross, with the infrared sensors scanning three hundreds sixty-degrees around him.

It was time-consuming. Even with the suit's servomotors and propulsion units, motion across the ice, against the buffeting wind, was a cumbersome business. But Massan continued to work his way across the iceberg, fighting down a gnawing, growing fear that Odal was not there at all.

And then he caught just the barest flicker of a shadow on his detector. Something, or someone, had darted behind a jutting rise of the ice, off by the edge of the iceberg.

Slowly and carefully, Massan made his way toward the base of the rise. He picked one of the oxy-bombs from his belt and held it in his right-hand claw.

Massan edged around the base of the ice cliff, and stood on a narrow ledge between the cliff and the churning sea. He saw no one. He extended the detector's range to maximum, and worked the scanners up the sheer face of the cliff toward the top.

There he was! The shadowy outline of a man etched itself on the detector screen. And at the same time, Massan heard a muffled roar, then a rumbling, crashing noise, growing quickly louder and more menacing.

He looked up the face of the ice cliff and saw a small avalanche of ice tumbling, sliding, growling toward him. *That devil set off a bomb at the top of the cliff!*

Massan tried to back out of the way, but it was too late. The first chunk of ice bounced harmlessly off his helmet, but the others knocked him off-balance so repeatedly that the servos had no chance to recover. He staggered blindly for a few moments, as more and more ice cascaded down on him, and then toppled off the ledge into the boiling sea.

Relax! he ordered himself. *Do not panic! The suit will float you. The servos will keep you right-side-up. You cannot be killed accidentally; Odal must perform the coup-de-grace himself.*

Then he remembered the emergency rocket units in the back of his suit. If he could orient himself properly, a touch of a control stud on his belt would set them off, and he would be boosted back onto the iceberg. He turned slightly inside the suit and tried to judge the iceberg's distance through the infrared detector. It was difficult, especially since he was bobbing madly in the churning currents.

Finally he decided to fire the rocket and make final adjustments of distance and landing site after he was safely out of the sea.

But he could not move his hand.

He tried, but his entire right arm was locked fast. He could not budge it an inch. And the same for the left. Something, or someone, was clamping his arms tight. He could not even pull them out of their sleeves.

Massan thrashed about, trying to shake off whatever it was. No use.

Then his detector screen was lifted slowly from the viewplate. He felt something vibrating on his helmet. The oxygen tubes! They were being disconnected.

He screamed and tried to fight free. No use. With a hiss, the oxygen tubes pulled free of his helmet. Massan could feel the blood pounding through his veins as he fought desperately to free himself.

Now he was being pushed down into the sea. He screamed again and tried to wrench his body away. The frothing sea filled his viewplate. He was under. He was being held under. And now ... now the viewplate itself was being loosened.

No! Don't! The scalding cold methane ammonia sea seeped in through the opening viewplate.

"It's only a dream!" Massan shouted to himself. "Only a dream. A dream. A—"

CHAPTER XI

Dr. Leoh stared at the dinner table without really seeing it. Coming to the restaurant had been Hector's idea. Three hours earlier, Massan had been removed from the dueling machine—dead.

Leoh sat stolidly, hands in lap, his mind racing in many different directions at once. Hector was off at the phone, getting the latest information from the meditechs. Odal had expressed his regrets perfunctorily, and then left for the Kerak Embassy, under a heavy escort of his own plainclothes guards. The government of the Acquataine Cluster was quite literally falling apart, with no man willing to assume responsibility ... and thereby expose himself. One hour after the duel, Kanus' troops had landed on all the major planets of the Szarno Confederacy; the annexation was a *fait accompli*.

And what have I done since I arrived on Acquatainia? Leoh demanded of himself. *Nothing. Absolutely nothing. I have sat back like a doddering old professor and played academic games with the machine, while younger, more vigorous men have USED the machine to suit their purposes.*

Used the machine. There was a fragment of an idea in that phrase. Something nebulous, that must be approached carefully or it will fade away. Used the machine, ... used it ... Leoh toyed with the phrase for a few moments then gave it up with a sigh of resignation. *Lord, I'm too tired even to think.*

Leoh focused his attention on his surroundings and scanned the busy dining room. It was a beautiful place, really; decorated with crystal and genuine woods and fabric draperies. Not a synthetic in sight. The waiters and cooks and busboys were humans, not the autocookers and servers that most restaurants employed. Leoh suddenly felt touched at Hector's attempt to restore his spirits—even if it was being done at Star Watch expense.

He saw the young Watchman approaching the table, coming back from the phone. Hector bumped two waiters and stumbled over a chair before reaching the relative safety of his own seat.

"What's the verdict?" Leoh asked.

Hector's lean face was bleak. "Couldn't revive him. Cerebral hemorrhage, the meditechs said—induced by shock."

"Shock?"

"That's what they said. Something must've, uh, overloaded his nervous system ... I guess."

Leoh shook his head. "I just don't understand any of this. I might as well admit it. I'm no closer to an answer now than I was when I arrived here. Perhaps I should have retired years ago, before the dueling machine was invented."

"Nonsense."

"No, I mean it." Leoh said. "This is the first real intellectual puzzle I've had to contend with in years. Tinkering with machinery ... that's easy. You know what you want, all you need is to make the machinery perform properly. But this ... I'm afraid I'm too old to handle a real problem like this."

Hector scratched his nose thoughtfully, then answered, "If you can't handle the problem, sir, then we're going to have a war on our hands in a matter of weeks. I mean, Kanus won't be satisfied with swallowing the Szarno group ... the Acquataine Cluster is next ... and he'll have to fight to get it."

"Then the Star Watch can step in," Leoh said, resignedly.

"Maybe ... but it'll take time to mobilize the Star Watch ... Kanus can move a lot faster than we can. Sure, we could throw in a task force ... a token group, that is. But Kanus' gang will chew them up pretty quick. I ... I'm no politician, sir, but I think I can see what will happen. Kerak will gobble up the Acquataine Cluster ... a Star Watch task force will be wiped out in the battle ... and we'll end up with Kerak at war with the Terran Commonwealth. And it'll be a real war ... a big one."

Leoh began to answer, then stopped. His eyes were fixed on the far entrance of the dining room. Suddenly every murmur in the busy room stopped dead. Waiters stood still between tables. Eating, drinking, conversation hung suspended.

Hector turned in his chair and saw at the far entrance the slim, stiff, blue-uniformed figure of Odal.

The moment of silence passed. Everyone turned to his own business and avoided looking at the Kerak major. Odal, with a faint smile on his thin face, made his way slowly to the table where Hector and Leoh were sitting.

They rose to greet him and exchanged perfunctory salutations. Odal pulled up a chair and sat with them.

"I assume that you've been looking for me," Leoh said. "What do you wish to say?"

Before Odal could answer, the waiter assigned to the table walked up, took a position where his back would be to the Kerak major, and asked firmly, "Your dinner is ready gentlemen. Shall I serve it now?"

Leoh hesitated a moment, then asked Odal, "Will you join us?"

"I'm afraid not."

"Serve it now," Hector said. "The major will be leaving shortly."

Again the tight grin broke across Odal's face. The waiter bowed and left.

"I have been thinking about our conversation of last night," Odal said to Leoh.

"Yes?"

"You accused me of cheating in my duels."

Leoh's eyebrows arched. "I said someone was cheating, yes—"

"An accusation is an accusation."

Leoh said nothing.

"Do you withdraw your words, or do you still accuse me of deliberate murder? I am willing to allow you to apologize and leave Acquatainia in peace."

Hector cleared his throat noisily. "This is no place to have an argument ... besides, here comes our dinner."

Odal ignored the Watchman. "You heard me, professor. Will you leave? Or do you accuse me of murdering Massan this afternoon?"

"I—"

Hector banged his fist on the table and jerked up out of his chair—just as the waiter arrived with a large tray of food. There was a loud crash. A tureen of soup, two bowls of salad, glasses, assorted rolls, vegetables, cheeses and other delicacies cascaded over Odal.

The Kerak major leaped to his feet, swearing violently in his native tongue. He sputtered back into basic Terran: "You clumsy, stupid oaf! You maggot-brained misbegotten peasant-faced—"

Hector calmly picked a salad leaf from the sleeve of his tunic. Odal abruptly stopped his tirade.

"I am clumsy," Hector said, grinning. "As for being stupid, and the rest of it, I resent that. I am highly insulted."

A flash of recognition lighted Odal's eyes. "I see. Of course. My quarrel here is not with you. I apologize." He turned back to Leoh, who was also standing now.

"Not good enough," Hector said. "I don't, uh, like the ... tone of your apology."

Leoh raised a hand, as if to silence the younger man.

"I apologized; that is sufficient." Odal warned.

Hector took a step toward Odal. "I guess I could insult your glorious leader, or something like that ... but this seems more direct." He took the water pitcher from the table and poured it calmly and carefully over Odal's head.

A wave of laughter swept the room. Odal went white. "You are determined to die." He wiped the dripping water from his eyes. "I will meet you before the week is out. And you have saved no one." He turned on his heel and stalked out.

"Do you realize what you've done?" Leoh asked, aghast.

Hector shrugged. "He was going to challenge you—"

"He will still challenge me, after you're dead."

"Uu-m-m, yes, well, maybe so. I guess you're right—Well, anyway, we've gained a little more time."

"Four days." Leoh shook his head. "Four days to the end of the week. All right, come on, we have work to do."

Hector was grinning broadly as they left the restaurant. He began to whistle.

"What are you so happy about?" Leoh grumbled.

"About you, sir. When we came in here, you were, uh, well ... almost beaten. Now you're right back in the game again."

Leoh glanced at the Star Watchman. "In your own odd way, Hector, you're quite a boy ... I think."

CHAPTER XII

Their groundcar glided from the parking building to the restaurant's entrance ramp, at the radio call of the doorman. Within minutes, Hector and Leoh were cruising through the city, in the deepening shadows of night.

"There's only one man," Leoh said, "who has faced Odal and lived through it."

"Dulaq," Hector agreed. "But ... for all the information the medical people have been able to get from him, he might as well be, uh, dead."

"He's still completely withdrawn?"

Hector nodded. "The medicos think that ... well, maybe in a few months, with drugs and psychotherapy and all that ... they might be able to bring him back."

"It won't be soon enough. We've only got four days."

"I know."

Leoh was silent for several minutes. Then: "Who is Dulaq's closest living relative? Does he have a wife?"

"I think his wife is, uh, dead. Has a daughter though. Pretty girl. Bumped into her in the hospital once or twice—"

Leoh smiled in the darkness. Hector's term, "bumped into" was probably completely literal.

"Why are you asking about Dulaq's next-of-kin?"

"Because," Leoh replied, "I think there might be a way to make Dulaq tell us what happened during his duel. But it is a very dangerous way. Perhaps a fatal way."

"Oh."

They lapsed into silence again. Finally he blurted, "Come on, my boy, let's find the daughter and talk to her."

"Tonight?"

"Now."

She certainly is a pretty girl, Leoh thought as he explained very carefully to Geri Dulaq what he proposed to do. She sat quietly and politely in the spacious living room of the Dulaq residence. The glittering chandelier cast touches of fire on her chestnut hair. Her slim body was slightly rigid with tension, her hands were clasped in her lap. Her face—which looked as though it could be very expressive—was completely serious now.

"And that is the sum of it," Leoh concluded. "I believe that it will be possible to use the dueling machine itself to examine your father's thoughts and determine exactly what took place during his duel against Major Odal!"

She asked softly, "But you are afraid that the shock might be repeated, and this could be fatal to my father?"

Leoh nodded wordlessly.

"Then I am very sorry, sir, but I must say no." Firmly.

"I understand your feelings," Leoh replied, "but I hope you realize that unless we can stop Odal and Kanus immediately, we may very well be faced with war."

She nodded. "I know. But you must remember that we are speaking of my father, of his very life. Kanus will have his war in any event, no matter what I do."

"Perhaps," Leoh admitted. "Perhaps."

Hector and Leoh drove back to the University campus and their quarters in the dueling machine chamber. Neither of them slept well that night.

The next morning, after an unenthusiastic breakfast, they found themselves standing in the antiseptic-white chamber, before the looming, impersonal intricacy of the machine.

"Would you like to practice with it?" Leoh asked.

Hector shook his head. "Maybe later."

The phone chimed in Leoh's office. They both went in. Geri Dulaq's face showed on the tri-di screen.

"I have just heard the news. I did not know that Lieutenant Hector has challenged Odal." Her face was a mixture of concern and reluctance.

"He challenged Odal," Leoh answered, "to prevent the assassin from challenging me."

"Oh—You are a very brave man, lieutenant."

Hector's face went through various contortions and slowly turned a definite red, but no words issued from his mouth.

"Have you reconsidered your decision?" Leoh asked.

The girl closed her eyes briefly, then said flatly, "I am afraid I cannot change my decision. My father's safety is my first responsibility. I am sorry."

They exchanged a few meaningless trivialities—with Hector still thoroughly tongue-tied and ended the conversation on a polite but strained note.

Leoh rubbed his thumb across the phone switch for a moment, then turned to Hector. "My boy, I think it would be a good idea for you to go straight to the hospital and check on Dulaq's condition."

"But ... why—"

"Don't argue, son. This could be vitally important."

Hector shrugged and left the office. Leoh sat down at his desk and drummed his fingers on the top of it. Then he burst out of the office and began pacing the big chamber. Finally, even that was too confining. He left the building and started stalking through the campus. He walked past a dozen buildings, turned and strode as far as the decorative fence that marked the end of the main campus, ignoring students and faculty alike.

Campuses are all alike, he muttered to himself, *on every human planet, for all the centuries there have been universities. There must be some fundamental reason for it.*

Leoh was halfway back to the dueling machine facility when he spotted Hector walking dazedly toward the same building. For once, the Watchman was not whistling. Leoh cut across some lawn and pulled up beside the youth.

"Well?" he asked.

Hector shook his head, as if to clear away an inner fog. "How did you know she'd be at the hospital?"

"The wisdom of age. What happened?"

"She kissed me. Right there in the hallway of the—"

"Spare me the geography," Leoh cut in. "What did she say?"

"I bumped into her in the hallway. We, uh, started talking ... sort of. She seemed, well ... worried about me. She got upset. Emotional. You know? I guess I looked pretty forlorn and frightened. I am ... I guess. When you get right down to it, I mean."

"You aroused her maternal instinct."

"I ... I don't think it was that ... exactly. Well, anyway, she said that if I was willing to risk my life to save yours, she couldn't protect her father any more. Said she was doing it out of selfishness, really, since he's her only living relative. I don't believe she meant that, but she said it anyway."

They had reached the building by now. Leoh grabbed Hector's arm and steered him clear of a collision with the half-open door.

"She's agreed to let us put Dulaq in the dueling machine?"

"Sort of."

"Eh?"

"The medical staff doesn't want him to be moved from the hospital ... especially not back to here. She agrees with them."

Leoh snorted. "All right. In fact, so much the better. I'd rather not have the Kerak people see us bring Dulaq to the dueling machine. So instead, we shall smuggle the dueling machine to Dulaq!"

CHAPTER XIII

They plunged to work immediately. Leoh preferred not to inform the regular staff of the dueling machine about their plan, so he and Hector had to work through the night and most of the next morning. Hector barely understood what he was doing, but with Leoh's supervision, he managed to dismantle part of the dueling machine's central network, insert a few additional black boxes that the professor had conjured up from the spare parts bins in the basement, and then reconstruct the machine so that it looked exactly the same as before they had started.

In between his frequent trips to oversee Hector's work, Leoh had jury-rigged a rather bulky headset and a hand-sized override control circuit.

The late morning sun was streaming through the tall windows when Leoh finally explained it all to Hector.

"A simple matter of technological improvisation," he told the bewildered Watchman. "You have installed a short-range transceiver into the machine, and this headset is a portable transceiver for Dulaq. Now he can sit in his hospital bed and still be 'in' the dueling machine."

Only the three most trusted members of the hospital staff were taken into Leoh's confidence, and they were hardly enthusiastic about Leoh's plan.

"It is a waste of time," said the chief psychophysician, shaking his white-maned head vigorously. "You cannot expect a patient who has shown no positive response to drugs and therapy to respond to your machine."

Leoh argued, Geri Dulaq coaxed. Finally the doctors agreed. With only two days remaining before Hector's duel with Odal, they began to probe Dulaq's mind. Geri remained by her father's bedside while the three doctors fitted the cumbersome transceiver to Dulaq's head and attached the electrodes for the automatic hospital equipment that monitored his physical condition. Hector and Leoh remained at the dueling machine, communicating with the hospital by phone.

Leoh made a final check of the controls and circuitry, then put in the last call to the tense little group in Dulaq's room. All was ready.

He walked out to the machine, with Hector beside him. Their footsteps echoed hollowly in the sepulchral chamber. Leoh stopped at the nearer booth.

"Now remember," he said, carefully, "I will be holding the emergency control unit in my hand. It will stop the duel the instant I set it off. However, if something should go wrong, you must be prepared to act quickly. Keep a close watch on my physical condition; I've shown you which instruments to check on the control board—"

"Yes sir."

Leoh nodded and took a deep breath. "Very well then."

He stepped into the booth and sat down. The emergency control unit rested on a shelf at his side; he took it in his hands. He leaned back and waited for the semi-hypnotic effect to take hold. Dulaq's choice of this very city and the stat-wand were known. But beyond that, everything was locked and sealed in Dulaq's subconscious mind. Could the machine reach into that subconscious, probe past the lock and seal of catatonia, and stimulate Dulaq's mind into repeating the duel?

Slowly, lullingly, the dueling machine's imaginary yet very real mists enveloped Leoh. When the mists cleared, he was standing on the upper pedestrian level of the main commercial street of the city. For a long moment, everything was still.

Have I made contact? Whose eyes am I seeing with, my own or Dulaq's?

And then he sensed it—an amused, somewhat astonished marveling at the reality of the illusion. Dulaq's thoughts!

Make your mind a blank, Leoh told himself. *Watch. Listen. Be passive.*

He became a spectator, seeing and hearing the world through Dulaq's eyes and ears as the Acquatainian Prime Minister advanced through his nightmarish ordeal. He felt the confusion, frustration, apprehension and growing terror as, time and again, Odal appeared in the crowd—only to melt into someone else and escape.

The first part of the duel ended, and Leoh was suddenly buffeted by a jumble of thoughts and impressions. Then the thoughts slowly cleared and steadied.

Leoh saw an immense and totally barren plain. Not a tree, not a blade of grass; nothing but bare, rocky ground stretching in all directions to the horizon and a disturbingly harsh yellow sky. At his feet was the weapon Odal had chosen. A primitive club.

He shared Dulaq's sense of dread as he picked up the club and hefted it. Off on the horizon he could see a tall, lithe figure holding a similar club walking toward him.

Despite himself, Leoh could feel his own excitement. He had broken through the shock-created armor that Dulaq's mind had erected! Dulaq was reliving the part of the duel that had caused the shock.

Reluctantly, he advanced to meet Odal. But as they drew closer together, the one figure of his opponent seemed to split apart. Now there were two, four, six of them. Six Odals, six mirror images, all armed with massive, evil clubs, advancing steadily on him.

Six tall, lean, blond assassins, with six cold smiles on their intent faces.

Horrified, completely panicked, he scrambled away, trying to evade the six opponents with the half-dozen clubs raised and poised to strike.

Their young legs and lungs easily outdistanced him. A smash on his back sent him sprawling. One of them kicked his weapon away.

They stood over him for a malevolent, gloating second. Then six strong arms flashed down, again and again, mercilessly. Pain and blood, screaming agony, punctuated by the awful thudding of solid clubs hitting fragile flesh and bone, over and over again, endlessly.

Everything went blank.

Leoh opened his eyes and saw Hector bending over him.

"Are you all right, sir?"

"I ... I think so."

"The controls all hit the danger mark at once. You were ... well, sir, you were screaming."

"I don't doubt it," Leoh said.

They walked, with Leoh leaning on Hector's arm, from the dueling machine booth to the office.

"That was ... an experience." Leoh said, easing himself onto the couch.

"What happened? What did Odal do? What made Dulaq go into shock? How does—"

The old man silenced Hector with a wave of his hand, "One question at a time, please."

Leoh leaned back on the deep couch and told Hector every detail of both parts of the duel.

"Six Odals," Hector muttered soberly, leaning back against the doorframe. "Six against one."

"That's what he did. It's easy to see how a man expecting a polite, formal duel can be completely shattered by the viciousness of such an attack. And the machine amplifies every impulse, every sensation."

"But how does he do it?" Hector asked, his voice suddenly loud and demanding.

"I've been asking myself the same question. We've checked over the dueling machine time and again. There is no possible way for Odal to plug in five helpers ... unless—"

"Unless?"

Leoh hesitated, seemingly debating with himself. Finally he nodded his head sharply, and answered. "Unless Odal is a telepath."

"Telepath? But—"

"I know it sounds farfetched. But there have been well-documented cases of telepathy for centuries throughout the Commonwealth."

Hector frowned. "Sure, everybody's heard about it ... natural telepaths ... but they're so unpredictable ... I don't see how—"

Leoh leaned forward on the couch and clasped his hands in front of his chin. "The Terran races have never developed telepathy, or any of the extrasensory talents. They never had to, not with tri-di communications and superlight starships. But perhaps the Kerak people are different—"

Hector shook his head. "If they had uh, telepathic abilities, they would be using them everywhere. Don't you think?"

"Probably so. But only Odal has shown such an ability, and only ... *of course!*"

"What?"

"Odal has shown telepathic ability only in the dueling machine."

"As far as we know."

"Certainly. But look, supposed he's a natural telepath ... the same as a Terran. He has an erratic, difficult-to-control talent. Then he gets into a dueling machine. The machine amplifies his thoughts. And it also amplifies his talent!"

"Ohhh."

"You see ... outside the machine, he's no better than any wandering fortune-teller. But the dueling machine gives his natural abilities the amplification and reproducibility that they could never have unaided."

Hector nodded.

"So it's fairly straightforward matter for him to have five associates in the Kerak Embassy sit in on the duel, so to speak. Possibly they are natural telepaths also, but they needn't be."

"They just, uh, pool their minds with his, hm-m-m? Six men show in the duel ... pretty nasty." Hector dropped into the desk chair.

"So what do we do now?"

"Now?" Leoh blinked at his young friend. "Why ... I suppose the first thing we should do is call the hospital and see how Dulaq came through."

Leoh put the call through. Geri Dulaq's face appeared on the screen.

"How's your father?" Hector blurted.

"The duel was too much for him," she said blankly. "He is dead."

"No," Leoh groaned.

"I ... I'm sorry," Hector said. "I'll be right down there. Stay where you are."

The young Star Watchman dashed out of the office as Geri broke the phone connection. Leoh stared at the blank screen for a few moments, then leaned far back in the couch and closed his eyes. He was suddenly exhausted, physically and emotionally. He fell asleep, and dreamed of men dead and dying.

Hector's nerve-shattering whistling woke him up. It was full night outside.

"What are you so happy about?" Leoh groused as Hector popped into the office.

"Happy? Me?"

"You were whistling."

Hector shrugged. "I always whistle, sir. Doesn't mean I'm happy."

"All right," Leoh said, rubbing his eyes. "How did the girl take her father's death?"

"Pretty hard. Cried a lot."

Leoh looked at the younger man. "Does she blame ... me?"

"You? Why, no sir. Why should she? Odal ... Kanus ... the Kerak Worlds. But not you."

The old professor sighed, relieved. "Very well. Now then, we have much work to do, and little more than a day in which to finish it."

"What do you want me to do?" Hector asked.

"Phone the Star Watch Commander—"

"My commanding officer, all the way back at Alpha Perseus VI? That's a hundred light-years from here."

"No, no, no." Leoh shook his head. "The Commander-in-Chief, Sir Harold Spencer. At Star Watch Central Headquarters. That's several hundred parsecs from here. But get through to him as quickly as possible."

With a low whistle of astonishment, Hector began punching buttons on the phone switch.

CHAPTER XIV

The morning of the duel arrived, and precisely at the agreed-upon hour, Odal and a small retinue of Kerak representatives stepped though the double doors of the dueling machine chamber.

Hector and Leoh were already there, waiting. With them stood another man dressed in the black-and-silver of the Star Watch. He was a blocky, broad-faced veteran with iron-gray hair and hard, unsmiling eyes.

The two little groups of men knotted together in the center of the room, before the machine's control board. The white-uniformed staff meditechs emerged from a far doorway and stood off to one side.

Odal went through the formality of shaking hands with Hector. The Kerak major nodded toward the other Watchman. "Your replacement?" he asked mischievously.

The chief meditech stepped between them. "Since you are the challenged party, Major Odal, you have the first choice of weapon and environment. Are there any instructions or comments necessary before the duel begins?"

"I think not," Odal replied. "The situation will be self-explanatory. I assume, of course, that Star Watchmen are trained to be warriors and not merely technicians. The situation I have chosen is one in which many warriors have won glory."

Hector said nothing.

"I intend," Leoh said firmly, "to assist the staff in monitoring this duel. Your aides may, of course, sit at the control board with me."

Odal nodded.

"If you are ready to begin, gentleman," the chief meditech said.

Hector and Odal went to their booths. Leoh sat at the control console, and one of the Kerak men sat down next to him.

Hector felt every nerve and muscle tensed as he sat in the booth, despite his efforts to relax. Slowly the tension eased, and he began to feel slightly drowsy. The booth seemed to melt away....

He was standing on a grassy meadow. Off in the distance were wooded hills. A cool breeze was hustling puffy clouds across the calm blue sky.

Hector heard a snuffling noise behind him, and wheeled around. He blinked, then stared.

It had four legs, and was evidently a beast of burden. At least, it carried a saddle on its back. Piled atop the saddle was a conglomeration of which looked to Hector—at first glance—like a pile of junk. He went over to the animal and examined it carefully. The "junk" turned out to be a long spear, various pieces of armor, a helmet, sword, shield, battle-ax and dagger.

The situation I have chosen is one in which many warriors have won glory. Hector puzzled over the assortment of weapons. They came straight out of Kerak's Dark Ages. No doubt Odal had been practicing with them for months, even years. He may not need five helpers.

Warily, Hector put on the armor. The breastplate seemed too big, and he was somehow unable to tighten the greaves on his shins properly. The helmet fit over his head like an ancient oil can, flattening his ears and nose and forcing him to squint to see through the narrow eye-slit.

Finally, he buckled on the sword and found attachments on the saddle for the other weapons. The shield was almost too heavy to lift, and he barely struggled into the saddle with all the weight he was carrying.

And then he just sat. He began to feel a little ridiculous. *Suppose it rains?* he wondered. But of course it wouldn't.

After an interminable wait, Odal appeared, on a powerful trotting charger. His armor was black as space, and so was his animal. *Naturally*, Hector thought.

Odal saluted gravely with his great spear from across the meadow. Hector returned the salute, nearly dropping his spear in the process.

Then, Odal lowered the spear and aimed it—so it seemed to Hector—directly at the Watchman's ribs. He pricked his mount into a canter. Hector did the same, and his steed jogged into a bumping, jolting gallop. The two warriors hurtled toward each other from opposite ends of the meadow.

And suddenly there were six black figured roaring down on Hector!

The Watchman's stomach wrenched within him. Automatically he tried to turn his mount aside. But the beast had no intention of going anywhere except straight ahead. The Kerak warriors bore in, six abreast, with six spears aimed menacingly.

Abruptly, Hector heard the pounding of other hoof-beats right beside him. Through a corner of his helmet-slit he glimpsed at least two other warriors charging with him into Odal's crew.

Leoh's gamble had worked. The transceiver that had allowed Dulaq to make contact with the dueling machine from his hospital bed was now allowing five Star Watch officers to join Hector, even though they were physically sitting in a starship orbiting high above the planet.

The odds were even now. The five additional Watchmen were the roughest, hardiest, most aggressive man-to-man fighters that the Star Watch could provide on a one-day notice.

Twelve powerful chargers met head on, and twelve strong men smashed together with an ear-splitting CLANG! Shattered spears showered splinters everywhere. Men and animals went down.

Hector was rocked back in his saddle, but somehow managed to avoid falling off.

On the other hand, he could not really regain his balance, either. Dust and weapons filled the air. A sword hissed near his head and rattled off his shield.

With a supreme effort. Hector pulled out his own sword and thrashed at the nearest rider. It turned out to be a fellow Watchman, but the stroke bounced harmlessly off his helmet.

It was so confusing. The wheeling, snorting animals. Clouds of dust. Screaming, raging men. A black-armored rider charged into Hector, waving a battle-ax over his head. He chopped savagely, and the Watchmans's shield split apart. Another frightening swing—Hector tried to duck and slid completely out of the saddle, thumping painfully on the ground, while the ax cleaved the air where his head had been a split-second earlier.

Somehow his helmet had been turned around. Hector tried to decide whether to thrash around blindly or lay down his sword and straighten out the helmet. The problem was solved for him by the *crang!* of a sword against the back of his helmet. The blow flipped him into a somersault, but also knocked the helmet completely off his head.

Hector climbed painfully to his feet, his head spinning. It took him several moments to realize that the battle had stopped. The dust drifted away, and he saw that all the Kerak fighters were down—except one. The black-armored warrior took off his helmet and tossed it aside. It was Odal. Or was it? They all looked alike. *What difference does it make?* Hector wondered. *Odal's mind is the dominant one.*

Odal stood, legs braced apart, sword in hand, and looked uncertainly at the other Star Watchman. Three of them were afoot and two still mounted. The Kerak assassin seemed as confused as Hector felt. The shock of facing equal numbers had sapped much of his confidence.

Cautiously he advanced toward Hector, holding his sword out before him. The other Watchmen stood aside while Hector slowly backpedaled, stumbling slightly on the uneven ground.

Odal feinted and cut at Hector's arm. The Watchman barely parried in time. Another feint, at the head, and a slash into the chest; Hector missed the parry but his armor saved him. Grimly, Odal kept advancing. Feint, feint, crack! and Hector's sword went flying from his hand.

For the barest instant everyone froze. Then Hector leaped desperately straight at Odal, caught him completely by surprise, and wrestled him to the ground. The Watchman pulled the sword from his opponent's hand and tossed it away. But with his free hand, Odal clouted Hector on the side of the head and knocked him on his back. Both men scrambled up and ran for the nearest weapons.

Odal picked up a wicked-looking double-bladed ax. One of the mounted Star

Watchmen handed Hector a huge broadsword. He gripped it with both hands, but still staggered off-balance as he swung it up over his shoulder.

Holding the broadsword aloft, Hector charged toward Odal, who stood dogged, short-breathed, sweat-streaked, waiting for him. The broadsword was quite heavy, even for a two handed grip. And Hector did not notice his own battered helmet laying on the ground between them.

Odal, for his part, had Hector's charge and swing timed perfectly in his own mind. He would duck under the swing and bury his ax in the Watchman's chest. Then he would face the others. Probably with their leader gone, the duel would automatically end. But, of course, Hector would not really be dead; the best Odal could hope for now was to win the duel.

Hector charged directly into Odal's plan, but the Watchman's timing was much poorer than anticipated. Just as he began the downswing of a mighty broadsword stroke, he stumbled on the helmet. Odal started to duck, then saw that the Watchman was diving face-first into the ground, legs flailing, and that heavy broadsword was cleaving through the air with a will of its own.

Odal pulled back in confusion, only to have the wild-swinging broadsword strike him just above the wrist. The ax dropped out of his hand, and Odal involuntarily grasped the wounded forearm with his left hand. Blood seeped through his fingers.

He shook his head in bitter resignation, turned his back on the prostrate Hector, and began walking away.

Slowly, the scene faded, and Hector found himself sitting in the booth of the dueling machine.

CHAPTER XV

The door opened and Leoh squeezed into the booth.

"You're all right?"

Hector blinked and refocused his eyes on reality. "Think so—"

"Everything went well? The Watchmen got through to you?"

"Good thing they did. I was nearly killed anyway."

"But you survived."

"So far."

Across the room, Odal stood massaging his forehead while Kor demanded: "How could they possibly have discovered the secret? Where was the leak?"

"That is not important now," Odal said quietly. "The primary fact is that they have not only discovered our secret, but they have found a way of duplicating it."

"The sanctimonious hypocrites," Kor snarled, "accusing us of cheating, and then they do the same thing."

"Regardless of the moral values of our mutual behavior," Odal said dryly, "it is evident that there is no longer any use in calling on telepathically-guided assistants, I shall face the Watchman alone during the second half of the duel."

"Can you trust them to do the same?"

"Yes. They easily defeated my aides a few minutes ago, then stood aside and allowed the two of us to fight by ourselves."

"And you failed to defeat him?"

Odal frowned, "I was wounded by a fluke. He is a very ... unusual opponent. I cannot decide whether he is actually as clumsy as he appears to be, or whether he is shamming and trying to make me overconfident. Either way, it is impossible to predict his behavior. Perhaps he is also telepathic."

Kor's gray eyes became flat and emotionless. "You know, of course, how the Chancellor will react if you fail to kill this Watchman. Not merely defeat him. He must be killed. The aura of invincibility must be maintained."

"I will do my best," Odal said.

"He must be killed."

The chime that marked the end of the rest period sounded. Odal and Hector returned to the their booths. Now it was Hector's choice of environment and weapons.

Odal found himself enveloped in darkness. Only gradually did his eyes adjust. He saw that he was in a spacesuit. For several minutes he stood motionless, peering into the darkness, every sense alert, every muscle coiled for immediate action.

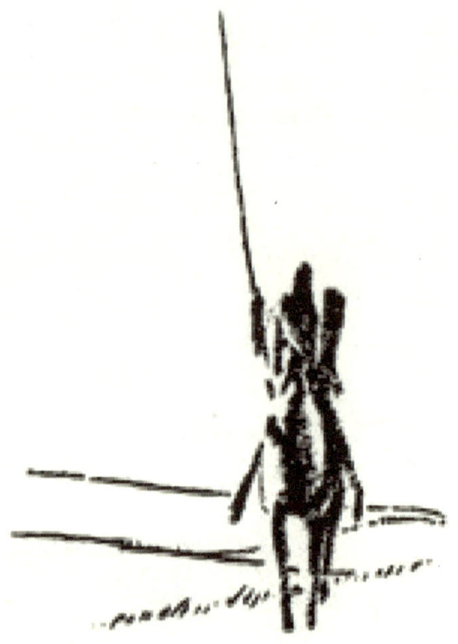

Dimly he could see the outlines of jagged rock against a background of innumerable stars. Experimentally, he lifted one foot. It stuck tackily, to the surface. *Magnetized boots*, Odal thought. *This must be a planetoid.*

As his eyes grew accustomed to the dimness, he saw that he was right. It was a small planetoid, perhaps a mile or so in diameter. Almost zero gravity. Airless.

Odal swiveled his head inside the fishbowl helmet of his spacesuit and saw, over his right shoulder, the figure of Hector—lank and ungainly even with the bulky suit. For a moment, Odal puzzled over the weapon to be used. Then Hector bent down, picked up a loose stone, straightened, and tossed it softly past Odal's head. The Kerak major watched it sail by and off into the darkness of space, never to return to the tiny planetoid.

A warning shot, Odal thought to himself. He wondered how much damage one could do with a nearly weightless stone, then remembered that inertial mass was unaffected by gravitational fields, or the lack of them. A fifty-pound rock might be easier to lift, but it would be just as hard to throw—and it would do just as much damage when it hit, regardless of its gravitational "weight."

Odal crouched down and selected a stone the size of his fist. He rose carefully, sighted Hector standing a hundred yards or so away, and threw as hard as he could.

The effort of his throw sent him tumbling off-balance, and the stone was far off-target. He fell to his hands and knees, bounced lightly and skidded to a stop. Immediately he drew his feet up under his body and planted the magnetized soles of his boots firmly on the iron-rich surface.

But before he could stand again, a small stone *pinged* lightly off his oxygen tank. The Star Watchman had his range already!

Odal scrambled to the nearest upjutting rocks and crouched behind them. *Lucky I didn't rip open the spacesuit*, he told himself. Three stones, evidently hurled in salvo, ticked off the top of the top of the rocks he was hunched behind. One of the stones bounced into his fishbowl helmet.

Odal scooped up a handful of pebbles and tossed them in Hector's general direction. That should make him duck. Perhaps he'll stumble and crack his helmet open.

Then he grinned to himself. That's it. Kor wants him dead, and that is the way to do it. Pin him under a big rock, then bury him alive under more rocks. A few at a time, stretched out nicely. While his oxygen supply gives out. That should put enough stress on his nervous system to hospitalize him, at least. Then he can assassinated by more conventional means. Perhaps he will even be as obliging as Massan, and have a fatal stroke.

A large rock. One that is light enough to lift and throw, yet also big enough to pin him for a few moments. Once he is down, it will be easy enough to bury him under more rocks.

The Kerak major spotted a boulder of the proper size, a few yards away. He backed toward it, throwing small stones in Hector's direction to keep the Watchman busy. In return, a barrage of stones began striking all around him. Several hit him, one hard enough to knock him slightly off-balance.

Slowly, patiently, Odal reached his chosen weapon—an oblong boulder, about the size of a small chair. He crouched behind it and tugged at it experimentally. It moved slightly. Another stone zinged off his arm, hard enough to hurt. Odal could see Hector clearly now, standing atop a small rise, calmly firing pellets at him. He smiled as he coiled, catlike, and tensed himself. He gripped the boulder with his arms and hands.

Then in one vicious uncoiling motion he snatched it up, whirled around, and hurled it at Hector. The violence of his action sent him tottering awkwardly as he released the boulder. He fell to the ground, but kept his eyes fixed on the boulder as it tumbled end over end, directly at the Watchman.

For an eternally-long instant Hector stood motionless, seemingly entranced. Then he leaped sideways, floating dreamlike in the low gravity, as the stone hurtled inexorably past him.

Odal pounded his fist on the ground in fury. He started up, only to have a good-sized stone slam against his shoulder, and knock him flat again. He looked up in time to see Hector fire another. The stone puffed into the ground inches from Odal's helmet. The Kerak major flattened himself. Several more stones clattered on his helmet and oxygen tank. Then silence.

Odal looked up and saw Hector squatting down, reaching for more ammunition. The Kerak warrior stood up quickly, his own fists filled with throwing stones. He cocked his arm to throw—

But something made him turn to look behind him. The boulder loomed before his eyes, still tumbling slowly, as it had when he had thrown it. It was too close and too big to avoid. It smashed into Odal, picked him off his feet and slammed against the upjutting rocks a few yards away.

Even before he started to feel the pain in his midsection, Odal began trying to push the boulder off. But he could not get enough leverage. Then he saw the Star Watchman's form standing over him.

"I didn't really think you'd fall for it," Odal heard Hector's voice in his ear-phones. "I mean ... didn't you realize that the boulder was too massive to escape completely after it had missed me? You could've calculated its orbit ... you just threw it into a, uh, six-minute orbit around the planetoid. It *had* to come back to perigee ... right where you were standing when you threw it, you know."

Odal said nothing, but strained every cell in his pain-wracked body to get free of the boulder. Hector reached over his shoulder and began fumbling with the valves that were pressed against the rocks.

"Sorry to do this ... but I'm not, uh, killing you, at least ... just defeating you. Let's see ... one of these is the oxygen valve, and the other, I think, is the emergency rocket pack ... now, which is which?" Odal felt the Watchman's hands searching for the proper valve. "I should've dreamed up suits without the rocket pack ... confuses things ... there, that's it."

Hector's hand tightened on a valve and turned it sharply. The rocket roared to life and Odal was hurtled free of the boulder, shot uncontrolled completely off the planetoid. Hector was bowled over by the blast and rolled halfway around the tiny chink of rock and metal.

Odal tried to reach around to throttle down the rocket, but the pain in his body was too great. He was slipping into unconsciousness. He fought against it. He knew he must return to the planetoid and somehow kill the opponent. But gradually the pain overpowered him. His eyes were closing, closing —

And, quite abruptly, he found himself sitting in the booth of the dueling ma-chine. It took a moment for him to realize that he was back in the real world. Then his thoughts cleared. He had failed to kill Hector.

And at the door of the booth stood Kor, his face a grim mask of anger.

CHAPTER XVI

The office was that of the new prime minister of the Acquataine Cluster. It had been loaned to Leoh for his conversation with Sir Harold Spencer. For the moment, it seemed like a great double room: half of it was dark, warm woods, rich draperies, floor-to-ceiling bookcases. The other half, from the tri-di screen onward, was the austere, metallic utility of a starship compartment.

Spencer was saying, "So this hired assassin, after killing four men and nearly wrecking a government, has returned to his native worlds."

Leoh nodded. "He returned under guard. I suppose he is in disgrace, or perhaps even under arrest."

"Servants of a dictator never know when they will be the ones who are served—on a platter." Spencer chuckled. "And the Watchman who assisted you, this Junior Lieutenant Hector, what of him?"

"He's not here just now. The Dulaq girl has him in tow, somewhere. Evidently it's the first time he's been a hero—"

Spencer shifted his weight in his chair. "I have long prided myself on the conviction that any Star Watch officer can handle almost any kind of emergency anywhere in the galaxy. From your description of the past few weeks, I was beginning to have my doubts. However, Junior Lieutenant Hector seems to have won the day ... almost in spite of himself."

"Don't underestimate him," Leoh said, smiling. "He turned out to be an extremely valuable man. I think he will make a fine officer."

Spencer grunted an affirmative.

"Well," Leoh said, "that's the complete story, to date. I believe that Odal is finished. But the Kerak Worlds have made good their annexation of the Szarno Confederacy, and the Acquataine Cluster is still very wobbly, politically. We haven't heard the last of Kanus—not by a long shot."

Spencer lifted a shaggy eyebrow. "Neither," he rumbled, "has he heard the last from us."

Lector House believes that a society develops through a two-fold approach of continuous learning and adaptation, which is derived from the study of classic literary works spread across the historic timeline of literature records. Therefore, we aim at reviving, repairing and redeveloping all those inaccessible or damaged but historically as well as culturally important literature across subjects so that the future generations may have an opportunity to study and learn from past works to embark upon a journey of creating a better future.

This book is a result of an effort made by Lector House towards making a contribution to the preservation and repair of original ancient works which might hold historical significance to the approach of continuous learning across subjects.

HAPPY READING & LEARNING!

LECTOR HOUSE LLP
E-MAIL: lectorpublishing@gmail.com